AN ANTIDOTE FOR DEATH?

Sir Lionel Barton was dead!
But who had sent the mysterious telegram to his old friend Dr. Petrie pleading that he come at once and: ". . . bring the antidote!"? What doctor in the world holds an antidote for death?

THE FIENDISH DR. FU MANCHU!

He had devised an antidote to the "living death." Had Barton fallen prey to that deadliest of all weapons in the evil doctor's diabolical arsenal?

But Fu Manchu was dead—or was he?
And where was his arch rival Nayland Smith in this time of need? These are the mysteries that Petrie and his colleagues attempt to solve, while unknowingly they pit their meager talents against the devastating beauty and inherent genius of

THE DAUGHTER OF FU MANCHU!

THE ADVENTURES OF
NAYLAND SMITH

•

DAUGHTER OF FU MANCHU

Sax Rohmer

PYRAMID BOOKS ▲ NEW YORK

DAUGHTER OF FU MANCHU

A PYRAMID BOOK

Published by arrangement with Doubleday & Company, Inc.

Pyramid edition published June 1964
  Third printing, February 1976

ISBN: 0-515-04024-X

Printed in the United States of America

Pyramid Books are published by Pyramid Communications, Inc.
Its trademarks, consisting of the word "Pyramid" and the por-
trayal of a pyramid, are registered in the United States Patent
Office.

PYRAMID COMMUNICATIONS, INC.
919 Third Avenue, New York, N.Y. 10022

CONTENTS

1 *THE LIVING DEATH*

JUST in sight of Shepheard's I pulled up.

I believe a sense of being followed is a recognized nervous disorder. But it was one I had never experienced without finding it to be based on fact.

Certainly what had occurred was calculated to upset the stoutest nerves. To lose an old and deeply respected friend, and in the very hour of the loss to be confronted by a mystery seemingly defying natural laws, is a test of staying power which any man might shirk.

I had set out for Cairo in a frame of mind which I shall not attempt to describe. But this damnable idea that I was spied upon—followed—asserted itself in the first place on the train.

In spirit still back in camp beside the body of my poor chief, I suddenly became conscious of queer wanderers in the corridor. One yellow face in particular I had detected peering in at me, which possessed such unusual and dreadful malignity that at some point just below Beni Suef I toured the cars from end to end determined to convince myself that those oblique squinting eyes were not a product of my imagination. Several times I had fallen into a semi-doze, for I had had no proper sleep for forty-eight hours.

I failed to find the yellow horror. This had disturbed me, because it made me distrust myself. But it served to banish my sleepiness. Reinforced with a stiff whisky-and-soda, I stayed very widely awake as the train passed

7

station after station in the Nile Valley and drew ever nearer to Cairo.

The squinting eyes did not reappear.

Then, having hailed a taxi outside the station, I suddenly became aware, in some quite definite way, that the watcher was following again. In sight of Shepheard's I pulled up, dismissed the taxi, and mounted the steps to the terrace.

Tables were prepared for tea, but few as yet were occupied. I could see no one I knew, but of this I was rather glad.

Standing beside one of those large ornamental vases at the head of the steps, I craned over, looking left along Sharia Kamel. I was just in time. My trick had its reward.

A limousine driven by an Arab chauffeur passed in a flash.

But the oblique squinting eyes of its occupant stared up at the balcony. It was the man of the train. I had not been dreaming.

I think he saw me, but of this I couldn't be sure. The car did not slacken speed and I lost sight of it at the bend by Esbekiyeh Gardens.

A white-robed, red-capped waiter approached. Mentally reviewing my condition and my needs, I ordered a pot of Arab coffee. I smoked a pipe, drank my coffee, and set out on foot for the club. Here I obtained the address I wanted. . . .

In a quiet thoroughfare a brass plate beside a courtyard entrance confirmed its correctness. In response to my ring a Nubian servant admitted me. I was led upstairs and without any ceremony shown into a large and delightfully furnished study.

The windows opened on a balcony draped with purple blossom and overhanging the courtyard where orange trees grew. There were many books and the place was full of flowers. In its arrangement, the rugs upon the floor, the ornaments, the very setting of the big writing table, I detected the hand of a woman. And I realized more keenly than ever what a bachelor misses and the price he pays for his rather overrated freedom.

My thoughts strayed for a moment to Rima, and I wondered, as I had wondered many many times, what I could have done to offend her. I was brought back sharply when I met the glance of a pair of steady eyes regarding me from beyond the big writing table.

The man I had come to see stood up with a welcoming smile. He was definitely a handsome man, gray at the temples and well set up. His atmosphere created an odd sense of security. In fact my first impression went far to explain much that I had heard of him.

"Dr. Petrie?" I asked.

He extended his hand across the table and I grasped it.

"I'm glad you have come, Mr. Greville," he replied. They sent me your message from the club." His smile vanished and his face became very stern. "Please try the armchair. Cigars in the wooden box, cigarettes in the other. Or here's a very decent pipe mixture"—sliding his pouch across the table.

"Thanks," I said; "a pipe, I think."

"You are shaken up," he went on—"naturally. May I prescribe?"

I smiled, perhaps a little ruefully.

"Not at the moment. I have been rather overdoing it on the train, trying to keep myself awake."

I filled a pipe whilst trying to muster my ideas. Then, glancing up, I met the doctor's steady gaze; and:

"Your news was a great shock to me," he said. "Barton, I know, was one of your oldest friends. He was also one of mine. Tell me—I'm all anxiety to hear."

At that I began,

"As you may have heard, Dr. Petrie, we are excavating what is known as Lafleur's Tomb at the head of the Valley of the Kings. It's a queer business and the dear old chief was always frightfully reticent about his aims. He was generous enough when a job was done and shared the credit more than fairly. But his sense of the dramatic made him a bit difficult. Therefore, I can't tell you very much about it. But two days ago he shifted the quarters, barred all approaches to the excavation, and generally behaved in a way which I knew from experience to mean that we were on the verge of some big discovery.

"We have two huts, but nobody sleeps in them. We are a small party and under canvas. But all this you will see for yourself—at least, I hope I can count on you? We shall have to rush for it."

"I am coming," Dr. Petrie replied quietly. "It's all arranged. God knows what use I can be. But since he wished it . . ."

"Some time last night," I presently went on, "I heard, or thought I heard, the chief call me: 'Greville! Greville!' His voice seemed strange in some way. I fell out of bed (it was pitch dark), jumped into slippers, and groped along to his tent."

I stopped. The reality and the horror of it stopped me. But at last:

"He was dead," I said. "Dead in his bed. A pencil had dropped from his fingers and the scribbling block which he used for notes lay on the floor beside him."

"One moment," Dr. Petrie interrupted me. "You say he was dead. Was this impression confirmed afterwards?"

"Forester, our chemist," I replied sadly, "is an M.R.-C.P. though he doesn't practise. The chief was dead. Sir Lionel Barton—the greatest Orientalist our old country has ever produced, Dr. Petrie. And he was so alive, so vital, so keen and enthusiastic."

"Good God!" Dr. Petrie murmured. "To what did Forester ascribe death?"

"Heart failure—a quite unsuspected weakness."

"Unaccountable! I could have sworn the man had a heart like an ox. But I am becoming somewhat puzzled, Mr. Greville. If Forester certified death from syncope, who sent me *this*?"

He passed a telegram across the table. I read it in growing bewilderment:

Sir Lionel Barton suffering catalepsy. Please come first train and bring antidote if any remains.

I stared at Petrie, then:

"No one in our camp sent it!" I said.

"What!"

"I assure you. No member of our party sent this message."

I saw that it had been delivered that morning and had been handed in at Luxor at six A.M. I began to read it aloud in a dazed way. And, whilst I was reading, a subdued but particularly eerie cry came from the courtyard. I stopped. It startled me. But its effect upon Dr. Petrie was amazing. He sprang up as though a shot had been fired in the room and leaped towards the open window.

§ 2

"WHAT was it?" I exclaimed.

Whilst the cry had not resembled any of the many with which I was acquainted in the land where the vendor of dates, of lemonade, of water, of a score of commodities has each his separate song, yet, though weird, it was not in itself definitely horrible.

Petrie turned, and:

"Something I haven't heard for ten years," he replied —and I saw with concern that he had grown pale— "which I had hoped never to hear again."

"What?"

"The signal used by a certain group of fanatics of Burma loosely known as Dacoits."

"Dacoits? But *Dacoity* in Burma has been dead for a generation!"

Petrie laughed.

"I made that very statement twelve years ago," he said. "It was untrue then. It is untrue now. Yet there isn't a soul in the courtyard."

And suddenly I realized that he was badly shaken. He was not the type of man who was readily unnerved, and I confess that the incident—trivial though otherwise it might have seemed—impressed me unpleasantly.

"Please God I am mistaken," he went on, walking back to his chair—"I must have been mistaken."

But that he was not, suddenly became manifest. The door opened and a woman came in, or rather—ran in.

I had heard men at the club rave about Dr. Petrie's wife, but the self-chosen seclusion of her life was such that up to this present moment I had never set eyes on her. I realized now that all I had heard was short of the truth. It is fortunate that modern man is un-affected by the Troy complex; for she was, I think, quite the most beautiful woman I had ever seen in my life. I shall not attempt to describe her, for I could only fail. But, seeing that she had not even noticed my existence, I wondered, as men will sometimes wonder, by what mystic chains Dr. Petrie held this unreally lovely creature.

She ran to him and he threw his arms about her.

"You heard it!" she whispered. "You heard it!"

"I know what you are thinking, dear," he said. "Yes, I heard it. But after all it isn't possible."

He looked across at me, and suddenly his wife seemed to realize my presence.

"This is Mr. Shan Greville," Petrie went on, "who brings me very sad news about our old friend, Sir Lionel Barton. I didn't mean you to know, yet. But . . ."

Mrs. Petrie conquered her fears and came forward to greet me.

"You are very welcome," she said.

She spoke English with a faint fascinating accent.

"But your news—do you mean——"

Into the beautiful eyes watching me I saw the strang-est expression creeping. It was questioning, doubting; fearful, analytical. And suddenly Mrs. Petrie turned from me to her husband, and:

"How did it happen?" she asked.

As she spoke the words, I thought she seemed to be listening.

Briefly, Dr. Petrie repeated what I had told him, concluding by handing his wife the mysterious telegram.

"If I may interrupt for a moment," I said, taking out my pocket case, "Sir Lionel must have written this at the moment of his fatal seizure. You see—it tails off. It was scribbled on the block which lay beside him. It was what brought me to Cairo."

I handed the pencilled message to Petrie. His wife bent over him as he read aloud, slowly:

"Not dead . . . Get Petrie . . . Cairo . . . amber . . . inject . . ."

She was facing me as he read—her husband could not see her face. But he saw the telegram slip from her fingers to the carpet.

"Kara!" he cried. "My dear! What is it?"

Her wonderful eyes, widely opened, were staring past me through the window out into the courtyard; and:

"*He* is alive!" she whispered. "O God! *He* is alive!"

I wondered if she referred to Sir Lionel; when suddenly she turned to Petrie, clutching the lapels of his coat and speaking eagerly, fearfully.

"Surely you understand? You *must* understand. That cry in the garden and now—this! It is the Living Death! It is the Living Death! He knew before it claimed him. '*Amber—inject.*'" She shook Petrie with a sudden passionate violence. "Think! . . . *The flask is in your safe.*"

And, watching Petrie's face, I realized that what had been unintelligible to me, to him had brought light.

"Merciful heavens!" he cried, and now I saw positive horror leap to his eyes. "Merciful heavens! I can't believe it—I *won't believe it.*"

He stared at me, a man distracted; and:

"Sir Lionel believed it," his wife said. "He wrote it. This is what he means."

And now I remembered those hideous oblique eyes which had looked in at me during my journey. I remembered the man in the car who had passed me at Shepheard's. Dacoits! Bands of Burmese robbers! I had thought of them as scattered. Apparently they were associated—a sort of guild. Sir Lionel knew the Far East almost better than he knew the Near East. So, suddenly I spoke—or rather I cried the words aloud:

"Do you mean, Mrs. Petrie, that you think he's been *murdered?*"

Dr. Petrie interrupted, and his reply silenced me.

"It's worse than that," he said.

If I had come to Cairo bearing a burden of sorrow, I thought, looking from the face of my host to the beautiful face of his wife, that my story had brought their happy world tumbling about them in dust.

§3

THE train to Luxor was full, but I had taken the precaution of booking accommodation before leaving the station. And, as I was later to learn, I had been watched!

I was frankly out of my depth. That Petrie was deeply concerned for his wife, who seemed now to be the victim of a mysterious terror, he was quite unable to conceal. The object locked in the safe referred to by Mrs. Petrie proved to be a glass flask sealed with wax and containing a very small quantity of what might, from its appearance, have been brandy. However, the doctor packed it up with care and placed it in his professional bag before leaving.

This, together with the feverish state of excitement into which I seemed to have thrown his household, was sufficiently mystifying. Coming on top of a tragedy and a sleepless night, it was almost the last straw.

Petrie explored the train as though he expected to find Satan in person on board.

"Are you looking for my cross-eyed man?" I asked.

"I am," he returned grimly.

And somehow, as his steady glance met mine, it occurred to me that he was hoping, and not fearing, to see the oblique-eyed spy. It dawned upon me that his fears were for his wife, left behind in Cairo, rather than for us. What in heaven's name was it all about?

However, I was too far gone to pursue these reflections, and long before the attendant had come to make the bed I fell fast asleep.

I was awakened by Dr. Petrie.

"I prescribe dinner," he said.

Feeling peculiarly cheap, I managed to make myself sufficiently presentable for the dining car, and presently sat down facing my friend, of whom I had heard so much and whom the chief had evidently regarded as a safe harbour in a storm.

A cocktail got me properly awake again and enabled me to define where troubled dreams left off and reality began. Petrie was regarding me with an expression compounded of professional sympathy and personal curiosity; and:

"You have had a desperately trying time, Greville," he said. "But you can't have failed to see that you have exploded a bombshell in my household. Now, before I say any more on the latter point, please bring me up to date. If there's been foul play, is there anyone you could even remotely suspect?"

"There is certainly a lot of mystery about our job," I confessed. "I know for a fact that Sir Lionel's rivals—I might safely call them enemies—have been watching him closely—notably Professor Zeitland."

"Professor Zeitland died in London a fortnight ago."

"What!"

"You hadn't heard? We had the news in Cairo. Therefore, *he* can be ruled out."

There was a short interval whilst the waiter got busy, and then:

"As I remember poor Barton," Petrie mused, "he was always surrounded by clouds of strange servants. Are there any in your camp?"

"Not a soul," I assured him. "We're a very small party. Sir Lionel, myself, Ali Mahmoud, the headman, Forester, the chemist—I have mentioned him before; and the chief's niece, Rima, who's our official photographer."

I suppose my voice changed when I mentioned Rima; for Petrie stared at me very hard, and:

"Niece?" he said. "Odd jobs women undertake nowadays."

"Yes," I answered shortly.

Petrie began to toy with his fish. Clearly his appetite was not good. It was evident that repressed excitement held him—grew greater with every mile of our journey.

"Do you know Superintendent Weymouth?" he asked suddenly.

"I've met him at the club," I replied. "Now that you mention it, I believe Forester knows him well."

"So do I," said Petrie, smiling rather oddly. "I've been trying to get in touch with him all day." He paused, then:

"There must be associations," he went on. "Some of you surely have friends who visit the camp?"

That question magically conjured up a picture before my mind's eye—the picture of a figure so slender as to merit the description serpentine, tall, languorous; I saw again the brilliant jade-green eyes, voluptuous lips, and those slim ivory hands nurtured in indolence. . . . Madame Ingomar.

"There is one," I began—I was interrupted.

The train had begun to slow into Wasta, and high above those curious discords of an Arab station, I had clearly detected a cry:

"Dr. Petrie! A message for Dr. Petrie."

He, too, had heard it. He dropped his knife and fork and his expression registered a sudden consternation.

§ 4

As PETRIE sprang to his feet, a tall figure in flying kit came rushing into the dining car, and:

"Hunter!" Petrie exclaimed. "Hunter!"

I, too, stood up in a state of utter bewilderment.

"What's the meaning of this?" Petrie went on.

He turned to me, and:

"Captain Jameson Hunter, of Imperial Airways," he explained—"Mr. Shan Greville."

He turned again to the pilot.

"What's the idea, Hunter?" he demanded.

"The idea is," the airman replied, grinning with evident enjoyment, "that I've made a dash from Heliopolis to cut you off at Wasta! Jump to it! You've got to be clear of the train in two minutes!"

"But we're in the middle of dinner!"

"Don't blame me. It's Superintendent Weymouth's doing. He's standing by where I landed the bus."

"But," I interrupted, "where are we going?"

"Same place," said the airman, grinning delightedly. "But I can get you there in no time, save you the Nile crossing and land you, I believe, within five hundred yards of the camp. Where's your compartment? You have to run for your things or leave them on the train. It doesn't matter much."

"It does," I said. I turned to Petrie. "I'll get your bag. Fix things with the attendant and meet me on the platform."

I rushed out of the dining car, observed in blank astonishment by every other occupant. Our compartment gained, I nearly knocked over the night attendant who was making the bed. Dr. Petrie's bag I grabbed at once. Coats, hats, and two light suitcases were quickly bundled out. I thrust some loose money into the hand of the badly startled attendant and made for the exit.

Petrie's bag I managed to place carefully on the platform. The rest of the kit I was compelled to throw out unceremoniously—for the train was already in motion. I jumped off the step and looked along the platform.

Far ahead, where the dining car had halted, I saw Petrie and Jameson Hunter engaged apparently in a heated altercation with the station master. Heads craned through many windows as the Luxor express moved off.

And suddenly, standing there with the baggage distributed about me, I became rigid, staring—staring—at a yellow, leering face which craned from a coach only one removed from that we had occupied.

The spy had been on the train!

I was brought to my senses by a tap on the arm. I turned. An airways mechanic stood at my elbow.

"Mr. Greville," he said, "is this your baggage?"

I nodded.

"Close shave," he commented. He began to pick up the bags. "I think I can manage the lot, sir. Captain Hunter will show you the way."

"Careful with the black bag!" I cried. "Keep it upright, and for heaven's sake, don't jolt it!"

"Very good, sir."

Hatless, dinnerless, and half asleep I stood, until Jameson Hunter, Dr. Petrie, and the station master joined me.

"It's all settled," said Hunter, still grinning cheerfully. "The station master here was rather labouring under the impression that it was a hold-up. I think he's been corrupted by American movies. Well, here we go!"

But the station master was by no means willing to let

us go. He was now surrounded by a group of subordinates, and above the chatter of their comments I presently gathered that we must produce our tickets. We did so, and pushed our way through the group. Further official obstruction was offered . . . when all voices became suddenly silent.

A big man, wearing a blue serge suit, extraordinarily reminiscent of a London policeman in mufti, and who carried his soft hat so that the moonlight silvered his crisp white hair, strolled into the station.

"Weymouth!" cried Petrie. "This is amazing! What does it mean?"

The big, genial man, whom I had met once or twice at the club, appeared to be under a cloud. His geniality was less manifest than usual. But the effect of his arrival made a splendid advertisement for the British tradition in Egypt. The station master and his subordinates positively wilted in the presence of this one-time chief inspector of the Criminal Investigation Department now in supreme command of the Cairo detective service.

Weymouth nodded to me, a gleam of his old cheeriness lighting the blue eyes; then:

"I don't begin to think what it means, Doctor," he replied, "but it was what your wife told me."

"The cry in the courtyard?"

"Yes. And the telegram I found waiting when I got back."

"Telegram?" Petrie echoed. He turned to me. "Did you send it, Greville?"

"No. Do you mean, Superintendent, you received a telegram from Luxor?"

"I do. I received one to-day."

"So did I," said Petrie, slowly. "Who, in sanity's name, sent those telegrams, Greville?"

But to that question I could find no answer.

"It's mysterious, I grant," said Weymouth. "But whoever he is, he's a friend. Mrs. Petrie thinks—"

"Yes," said Petrie, eagerly.

Weymouth smiled in a very sad way, and:

"She always knew in the old days," he added. "It was uncanny."

"It was," Petrie agreed.

"Well, over the phone to-night she told me—"

"Yes?"

"She told me she had the old feeling."

"Not—?"

"So I understood, Doctor. I didn't waste another minute. I phoned Heliopolis and by a great stroke of luck found Jameson Hunter there with a bus, commissioned to pick up an American party now in Assouan. He was leaving in the morning, but I arranged with him to leave to-night."

"Moonlight is bad for landing unless one knows the territory very well," Jameson Hunter interrupted. "Fortunately I knew of a good spot outside here, and I know another just behind Der-el-Bahari. If we crash, it will be a bad show for Airways."

We hurried out to where a car waited, Dr. Petrie personally carrying the bag with its precious contents; and soon, to that ceaseless tooting which characterizes Egyptian drivers, we were dashing through the narrow streets with pedestrians leaping like hares from right and left of our course.

Outside the town we ran into a cultivated area, but only quite a narrow belt. Here there was a road of sorts. We soon left this and were bumping and swaying over virgin, untamed desert. On we went, and on, in the bright moonlight. I seemed to have stepped over the borderline of reality. The glorious blaze of stars above me had become unreal, unfamiliar. My companions were unreal—a dream company.

All were silent except Jameson Hunter, whose constant ejaculations of "Jumping Jupiter!" when we took an unusually bad bump indicated that he at least had not succumbed to that sense of mystery which had claimed the rest of us.

On a long, gentle slope dangerously terminated by a ravine, the plane rested. Our baggage was quickly transferred from the car and we climbed on board. A second before the roar of the propeller washed out conversation:

"Hunter," said Weymouth, "stretch her to the full. It's a race to save a man from living death. . . ."

2 RIMA

IT WAS bumpy travelling and I had never been a good sailor. Jameson Hunter stuck pretty closely to the river but saved miles, of course, on the many long bends, notably on that big sweep immediately below Luxor, where, leaving the Nile Valley north of Farshût, we crossed fifty miles of practically arid desert, heading east-southeast for Kûrna.

I was in poor condition, what with lack of sleep and lack of meals; and I will not enlarge upon my state of discomfort beyond saying that I felt utterly wretched. Sometimes I dozed; and then Rima's grave eyes would seem to be watching me in that maddeningly doubtful way. Once I dreamed that the slender ivory hands of Madame Ingomar beckoned to me. . . .

I awoke in a cold perspiration. Above the roar of the propeller I seemed to hear her bell-like, hypnotic voice.
. . .

Who was this shadowy figure, feared by Petrie, by his wife—by Weymouth? What had he to do with the chief's sudden death? Were these people deliberately mystifying me, or were they afraid to tell me what they suspected?

Forester was convinced that Barton was dead. I could not doubt it. But in the incomprehensible message scribbled at the last, Petrie seemed to have discovered a hope which was not apparent to me. Weymouth's words had reinforced it.

"A race to save a man from living death."

Evidently he too, believed . . . believed what?

It was no sort of problem for one in my condition, but at least I had done my job quicker than I could have hoped. Luck had been with me.

Above all, my own personal experience proved that there was something in it. Who had sent the telegrams?

Who had uttered that cry in the courtyard? And why had I been followed to Cairo and followed back? Thank heaven, at last I had shaken off that leering, oblique-eyed spy.

Jameson Hunter searched for and eventually found the landing place which he had in mind—a flat, red-gray stretch east of the old caravan road.

I was past reliable observation, but personally I could see nothing of the camp. This perhaps was not surprising as it nestled at the head of a wâdi, represented from our present elevation by an irregular black streak.

However, I was capable of appreciating that the selected spot could not be more than half a mile west of it. Hunter brought off a perfect landing, and with a swimming head I found myself tottering to the door.

When I had scrambled down:

"Wait a minute," said Petrie. "Ah, here's my bag. You've been through a stiff time, Greville. I am going to prescribe."

His prescription was a shot of brandy. It did me a power of good.

"If we had known," said Hunter, "some sandwiches would have been a worthy effort. But the whole thing was so rushed—I hadn't time to think."

He grinned cheerfully.

"Sorry my Phantom-Rolls isn't here to meet us," he said. "Someone must have mislaid it. It's a case of hoofing, but the going's good."

Carrying our baggage, we set out in the moonlight. We had all fallen silent now, even Jameson Hunter. Only our crunching footsteps broke the stillness. I think there is no place in the world so calculated to impress the spirit of man as this small piece of territory surrounding those two valleys where the quiet dead of Egypt lie. At night, when the moon sails full, he would be a pitiful soul who, passing that way, failed to feel the touch of eternity.

For my own part, as familiar landmarks appeared, a dreadful unrest compounded of sorrow and hope began to take possession of me. Above all, selfishly no doubt, I asked myself again and again—had Rima returned?

We were not expected until morning when the Cairo train arrived. Consequently I was astounded when on mounting the last ridge west of the wâdi I saw Forester hurrying to meet us. Of course, I might have known, had I been capable of associating two ideas, that the sound of our approach must have aroused the camp.

Forester began to run.

Bad news casts a long shadow before it. I forgot my nausea, my weariness. It came to me like a revelation that something fresh had occurred—something even worse than that of which I had carried news to Cairo.

I was not alone in my premonition. I saw Weymouth grasp Petrie's arm.

Forester began shouting:

"Is that you, Greville? Thank God you've come!"

Now, breathless, he joined us.

"What is it?" I asked. "What else has happened?"

"Only this, old man," he panted. "We locked the chief's body in the big hut, as you remember. I had serious doubts about notifying the authorities. And to-night about dusk I went to . . . look at him."

He grasped me by both shoulders.

"Greville!" Even in the moonlight I could see the wildness in his eyes. "His body had vanished."

"What!" Weymouth yelled.

"There isn't a trace—there isn't a clue. He's just been spirited away!"

§ 2

"IF ONLY Nayland Smith could join us," said Weymouth.

Dr. Petrie, looking very haggard in the lamplight, stared at him.

"The same thought had just crossed my own mind," he replied. "I am due to sail for England on Thursday. I had been counting the days. He's meeting me in . . ."

I knew that I could never again be present at so singular a scene. The hut was in part a laboratory, one end being devoted to Forester's special province, and containing a table laden with jars, test tubes, and other chemical paraphernalia. In part it was a museum. There were plans, diagrams, and photographs—Rima's photographs—pinned on the walls: lumps of stone bearing labels stacked upon the floor; and in open cases were all sorts of fragments found during the earlier stages of our excavation and duly tabulated in the same way.

There was a very dilapidated mummy case at the further end of the hut, which we had taken over from the Egypt Exploration people and had not troubled to remove. The lid rested against the wall. Then there was a long, bare table, very stoutly built, upon which finds were stacked at the end of the day, examined, and sorted according to their value. This, particularly, was my job. But at the moment, as I have said, the table was empty. When I had seen it last before leaving for Cairo, the body of Sir Lionel Barton lay upon it, covered by a gray blanket.

Now, in almost complete silence, for twenty minutes or more, I had watched a one-time chief inspector of Scotland Yard carrying out a detailed investigation in that strangest of settings.

Weymouth had not confined his inquiries to the hut alone, but, assisted by a flash-lamp, had examined the lock of the door, the windows, the path outside; but had finally returned and stared at the table.

Now he fixed his eyes upon me, and:

"Mr. Greville," he said, "you are not prejudiced by certain suspicions of mine which are shared by Dr. Petrie. I asked Mr. Forester to see to the comfort of Jameson Hunter because I wanted just the three of us alone here. Now, you look pretty well whacked, but I know how you feel about this thing; so I am going to ask you a few questions."

"As many as you like," I replied.

Superintendent Weymouth sat down on the bench just beside the door and knitted his brows; then:

"Where is the headman Ali Mahmoud?" he asked.

"Forester tells me he sent him across to Luxor to-night with a letter for our friend the manager of the Winter Palace. Forester asked him, in the letter, to call you, Superintendent, in Cairo, and to explain what had happened. Ali should be back, now."

Weymouth nodded thoughtfully.

"Leaving out for the moment the circumstances of Sir Lionel's death," said he, "how long a time elapsed between your finding him in his tent and the removal of his body to this hut?"

"Roughly, two hours," I replied after a few moments' thought.

"During those two hours someone was always in sight of the tent?"

"Certainly."

"When was it decided he should be moved?"

"When I made up my mind to go to Cairo. I gave instructions for his body to be placed in this hut . . . I am second in command, you know. Forester agreed, although he swore that life was extinct. I personally superintended the job. I locked the hut, handed the keys to Forester, and turned in, hoping for some sleep before starting for Luxor."

"Did you sleep?"

"No. I lay awake right up to the time I had to set out."

"Did anything unusual occur during the night?"

I thought hard, and then:

"Yes," I replied. "There was a queer howling of dogs. Ali Mahmoud turned out. He said the sound had not been made by dogs. But of course he was rather strung up. We all were. We searched but found nothing."

"H'm! What time was this?"

"I am afraid I can't tell you. But some time before dawn."

"Did you open this hut?"

"No."

"Ah!" said Weymouth meditatively. "That was a pity. And now, Mr. Greville, there's another point I'm not clear about. You spoke of Sir Lionel's niece. Where is she and where was she at the time of the tragedy?"

I had expected the question, of course. Nevertheless I didn't quite know how to meet it. I saw Dr. Petrie regarding me curiously, and at last:

"I don't know where she is!" I replied—and recognized how strange the words must sound.

"What!" Weymouth exclaimed. "But I thought she was official photographer?"

"She is. But . . . Well! We had a quarrel. She went across to Luxor on Tuesday at midday. I haven't seen her since!"

"Oh, I see," said Weymouth. "Forgive me. I hadn't grasped the position. Sir Lionel knew of her absence?"

"He treated it as a joke. That was his way. She often stayed in Luxor and worked here during the day."

"Did he approve of the—understanding?"

"Yes. At least I think so."

"I suppose, as she hasn't come back, that she doesn't know what's happened?"

"I suppose so. But I am very anxious . . ."

"Naturally." Weymouth looked suddenly grave; and then:

"Perhaps, Mr. Greville," he said, "you would ask Forester to come in?"

I opened the door and walked out in the dense shadow of the wâdi. A new atmosphere invested it, an atmosphere to which, even mentally, I didn't like to give a name, but which nevertheless was an atmosphere of *terror*.

What was the meaning of the disappearance of Sir Lionel's body? Whom could it benefit? Most damnable mystery of all—what was the information clearly shared by Weymouth and Petrie which they were suppressing?

So my thoughts ran as I walked through the shadows. The moon was out of sight from the wâdi but the stars were wonderful. And suddenly the natural law of things had its way. I began to think of Rima, to the exclusion of everything else.

Her empty tent—the tent which she occupied when she spent the night in camp—was on the slope directly ahead. Moonlight touched it at one point, but the front was in shadow.

"If I am in the way," I seemed to hear her voice saying again, "I can go.—"

If she was in the way! What had she meant? I had had no chance to find out. She had gone. Undoubtedly she was labouring under some strange delusion. But where was she—and did she know what had happened?

I was abreast of her tent, now, and something—an empty longing, no doubt—prompted me to peep inside. As I did so, an incredible thing happened—or, rather, two incredible things.

The mournful howling of a dog arose, apparently quite close to the camp. And in the darkness of the tent something stirred!

I suppressed a cry, bent forward with outstretched arms . . . and found a slim soft body in my embrace!

Even then, I couldn't believe what was true, couldn't appreciate the nature of my capture, until:

"Shan! Shan!" came a stifled cry. "You're hurting me dreadfully!"

"Rima!" I exclaimed—and wondered if my heart or hers throbbed the more wildly.

I said not another word. Stooping, I kissed her with a desperation which probably sprang from a submerged fear that she would never give me an opportunity of kissing her again.

But, thank heaven, that doubt was groundless. She threw her arms around my neck, as the mournful howling died away, and:

"Shan," she said, "I'm terrified, Shan dear!"

But her kisses had given me the right to console her, and when we presently reverted to sanity:

"When did you arrive, darling?" I asked.

"I came back with Ali. He told me—everything about it. So, of course, I had to come."

"But what made you go?"

She nestled her adorable little tousled head against me.

"I won't be scolded," she said—"although I am to blame! No, please, Shan. I truly meant what I said. I did really think I was in the way."

"In whose way?"

"If you talk to me like that I won't answer. Besides, there isn't time now. I should have come back to-night even if I had had to come alone. I have something most extraordinary to tell you . . ."

But now came the sound of voices.

"I tell you it *wasn't* a dog," I heard Forester say.

"It *wasn't* either!" Rima whispered. "But you must go, Shan. I'm all right, now. Who is in the big hut?"

"Dr. Petrie and Superintendent Weymouth—"

"They were old friends . . . weren't they—"

"Yes, darling. Don't despair. It sounds absurd to say so, but they have a theory that the chief—"

"Please tell me."

"It's hardly fair, Rima. I don't believe it, myself. But they think he may be alive!"

She clung to me very tightly, and then:

"But I think so, too!" she whispered.

§3

"Do you know, Greville," said Forester. "I never liked this job. Lafleur's Tomb has a bad name."

We were walking back to the hut.

"What do you mean?"

"Well, you know as much as I do. Nobody has tackled it since Lafleur's time. But old Zeitland was planning to come out."

"He died recently in London."

"I know! And what about the Frenchman—"

"Do you mean Lafleur?"

"Yes, somewhere in 1908—or 1909, wasn't it? Well, I may be wrong"—Forester halted just as we reached the hut—"but didn't Lafleur disappear?"

I racked my memory for some moments. Lafleur was before my time and the facts were hazy. But at last:

"Yes," I replied slowly. "I believe there was some mystery, Forester. Though oddly enough it had never occurred to me before."

"It never occurred to *me* until we made that astounding discovery to-night. Why should it? But in view of what's happened, it's more than odd, don't you think?"

"We must tell Weymouth."

We went into the hut. Weymouth was sitting where I had left him, his brows still wrinkled in thought. . . . Dr. Petrie was pacing slowly up and down. As we entered, Weymouth raised his kindly blue eyes to Forester, and:

"Did you catch that dog?" he asked.

"No," said Forester, staring hard. "Did it sound like a dog to you?"

"It *wasn't* a dog," Weymouth replied simply. "This camp is being watched! Has anything occurred which might account for this signalling?"

"Yes," I broke in. "Ali Mahmoud has returned—and Rima Barton is with him."

"Ah!" Weymouth murmured. "I am glad to hear it. . . ."

"Greville and I have been thinking—" Forester began, when:

"One moment!" Weymouth raised his hand. "We shall get muddled. You can help me most, Forester, by letting me plod through the inquiry in my own way. I have the facts up to the time Mr. Greville left last night; now I want to know what happened afterwards."

"It's painfully simple," Forester replied. "Everything we might be likely to want was moved from here, naturally; so there was no occasion for anyone to enter the place. But deaths, of course, in the climate up here ought to be notified and dealt with promptly."

Weymouth nodded.

"Greville got me to agree to be quiet for the present, and nobody else knew, except Ali."

"You're sure nobody else knew? What about the men?"

"They live in Kûrna. None were in camp. We removed the chief in the darkness—didn't we, Greville?—and next morning I gave out that he had gone across to Luxor with Greville, here, and was proceeding down to Cairo. I stopped all work, of course."

"Yes, I see."

"At about dusk to-night—I should say last night—I thought it advisable to—er—inspect the body."

"Quite!"

"I opened the door, looked in, and . . . the hut was as you see it now."

"What about the blanket?"

"The blanket had disappeared, as well as the body."

"You're sure the door was locked?"

"Perfectly sure. I *unlocked* it."

"The window?"

"Fastened on the inside as you found it."

"Thank you," said Weymouth quietly.

He stared across at Dr. Petrie and there was a silence of some seconds' duration; a very odd silence, in which I sensed a mental communion going on between these two men, based upon some common knowledge which Forester and I didn't share. But at last it was broken by Dr. Petrie.

"Strangely like *his* handiwork!"

I began to be a bit ruffled. I thought the time had come for pooling the known facts. Indeed I was about to say so, when Weymouth spoke again.

"Was there anyone in the habit of visiting this camp?"

"No," said Forester. "The chief wouldn't allow a soul past the barriers." He stared across at me. "I except Madame Ingomar," he added. "But Greville can tell you more about the lady than I can."

"Why do you say that?" I cried angrily.

"Evidently because he thinks so," said Weymouth in a stern voice. "This is no time, gentlemen, for personal matters. You are assisting at an official inquiry."

"I am sorry," Forester replied. "My remark was quite out of place. The truth is, Superintendent, that neither Greville nor I know very much about Madame Ingomar. But she seemed to favour Greville's society, and we used to pull his leg about it. . . ."

My thoughts began to stray again. Had I been blind? And where I had been blind, had Rima seen?

"Who is this woman?"

Weymouth's tense query brought me back to the job in hand.

Forester laughed dryly, and:

"A question I have often put to Greville," he replied, "but which I know he was no more able to answer than anyone else, except the chief."

"Oh, I see. A friend of Sir Lionel's?"

I nodded. Weymouth was staring in my direction.

"What nationality?"

I shook my head blankly.

"I always said Hungarian," Forester declared. "Simply because of her name. Greville thought she was Japanese."

"Japanese!" Dr. Petrie rapped the word out with startling suddenness. "Why Japanese?"

"Well," said Forester, "it wasn't an unreasonable guess, because her eyes *did* slant slightly.'

Weymouth exchanged a rapid glance with Dr. Petrie and stood up.

"An attractive woman—young?" he challenged—for the words were spoken almost like a challenge.

"Undoubtedly," I replied. "Smart, cultured, and evidently well-to-do."

"Dark?"

"Very."

"What coloured eyes?"

"Jade-green," said Forester.

Again I detected a rapid exchange of glances between Petrie and Weymouth.

"Tall?" asked the former.

"Yes, unusually tall."

"An old friend of Sir Lionel's?"

"We were given to understand," said Forester, "that she was the widow of a certain Dr. Ingomar whom the chief knew well at one time."

"Was she staying at one of the Luxor hotels?" Weymouth asked.

"I'm afraid I can't tell you," I replied. "She wasn't staying at the Winter Palace."

"You mean neither of you know. Does Miss Barton know?"

"I have never asked her."

"When was she last here?"

"On Monday," Forester answered promptly—"the day the chief switched the quarters around and put up barricades."

"But did Sir Lionel never speak of her?" asked Dr. Petrie.

"No," I said. "He was a man who gave few confidences, as you are aware."

"Was there any suggestion of intimacy between them?" Weymouth was the speaker. "Did Sir Lionel show any jealousy, for instance?"

"Not that I ever noticed," Forester replied. "He

treated her as he treated everybody—with good-humoured tolerance! After all, the chief must have said good-bye to sixty, Weymouth!"

"Stranger things have happened," Petrie commented dryly. "I think, Weymouth, our next step is to establish the identity of this Madame Ingomar. Do you agree with me?"

"I do," said Weymouth, "absolutely"—and his expression had grown very grim.

He stared from me to Forester, and:

"You're both getting annoyed," he said. "I can see it. You know that the doctor here and I have a theory which we haven't shared with you. Very well, you shall know the facts. Ask Rima Barton to join us, and arm Ali Mahmoud. Tell him to mount guard and shoot anything he sees moving!"

"What on earth does this mean?" Forester demanded.

"It means," said Petrie, "that we are dealing with agents of Dr. Fu Manchu. . . ."

§4

DR. FU MANCHU! When that story was told, the story which Weymouth unfolded in the hut in the wâdi, whilst I can't answer for Forester, personally I was amazed beyond belief.

Rima's sweet face, where she sat half in shadow, was a fascinating study. She had ridden up from Kûrna with Ali Mahmoud. In the tent, when I had found her in my arms, she had worn riding kit; but now she had changed into a simple frock and had even made some attempt to straighten the tangle of her windblown hair. The night ride had whipped a wild colour into her tanned cheeks; her grave Irish eyes seemed even brighter than usual as she listened spellbound.

Some of the things Weymouth spoke of aroused echoes in my memory. I had been too young at the time to associate these events one with another. But I remembered having heard of them. I was considering the advantages of a legal calling when the war disturbed my promising career. The doings of this great and evil man, some of whose history I learned that morning, had reached me merely as rumours in the midst of altogether more personal business.

But now I grasped the fact that if these two clever and experienced men were correct in their theories, a veritable plague was about to be loosed upon the world.

Dr. Fu Manchu!

"Sir Lionel and I," said Dr. Petrie, "and Nayland Smith were last of those on the side of the angels to see him alive. It's possible he survived, but I am not prepared to believe it. What I am prepared to believe is that *some-one else* may be carrying on his work. What was a Dacoit —probably a Burman—a professional robber and murderer, doing in the courtyard of my house in Cairo last night? We know now, Greville, he was following *you*. But the cry points to an accomplice. He was not alone! The old net, Weymouth"—he turned to the latter—"closing round us again! Then—this camp is watched."

"I have said it before," Weymouth declared, "but I'll say it again; if only Nayland Smith could join us!"

"You refer of course, to Sir Denis Nayland Smith," said Forester, "one of the assistant commissioners at Scotland Yard? I know people who know him. Used to be a police official in Burma?"

"He did," Petrie replied. "He also saved the British Empire, by the way. But if we have many unknown enemies, we have at least one unknown friend."

"Who is that?" I asked.

"The well-informed stranger," Petrie replied, "who wired me in Cairo—and who wired Weymouth. Whoever he may be, he takes no chances. Dr. Fu Manchu was master of a method for inducing *artificial catalepsy*. It was one of the most dangerous weapons in his armoury. I alone, as I believe, possess a drop of the antidote. The man who sent that telegram knew this!"

"So much for unknown friends," said Weymouth. "As to unknown enemies, either you have a Dacoit amongst your workmen or there was a stranger in camp last night."

"You've found a clue!" Rima cried.

"I have, Miss Barton. There's only one fact of which

I have to make sure. If I am wrong in that, maybe all my theory falls down."

"What's the fact?" Forester asked, with an eagerness which told how deeply he was impressed.

"It's this," said Weymouth. He fixed a penetrating gaze upon me. "Was Sir Lionel completely undressed when you found him?"

"No," I replied promptly. "It was arranged that we all turned out at four to work on the job."

"Then he was fully dressed?"

"Not fully."

"Did he carry the key of this hut?"

"He carried all the keys on a chain."

"Was this chain on him when you found him?"

"Yes."

"Did you detach it?"

"No. We laid him here as we found him."

"Partially dressed?"

"Yes."

Weymouth slowly crossed to the mummy case at one end of the hut. The lid was detached and leaned against the wall beside the case.

"Both you, Greville," he went on, turning, "and Forester were present when Sir Lionel's body was brought in here?"

"Ali and I carried him," Forester returned shortly. "Greville supervised."

"Did Ali leave when *you* left?"

"He did."

"Good," Weymouth went on quietly. "But I am prepared to swear that not one of you looked into the recess behind this sarcophagus lid."

I stared blankly at Forester. He shook his head.

"We never even thought of it," he confessed.

"Naturally enough," said Weymouth. "Look what I found there."

A lamp stood on the long table; and now, taking a piece of paper from his pocket, and opening the paper under the lamp, the superintendent exposed a reddish, fibrous mass. Rima sprang forward and with Forester and myself bent eagerly over it. Petrie watched.

"It looks to me like a wad of tobacco," said Forester, "chewed by someone whose gums were bleeding!"

Petrie bent between us and placed a lens upon the table.

"I have examined it," he said. "Give me your opinion, Mr. Forester. As a physician you may recognize it."

Forester looked, and we all watched him in silence. I remember that I heard Ali Mahmoud coughing out in the wâdi and realized that he was keeping as close to human companionship that night as his sentry duties permitted.

Shrugging, Forester passed the glass to me. I peered in turn, but almost immediately laid the glass down.

Petrie looked at Forester; but:

"Out of my depth!" the latter declared. "It's vegetable; but if it's something tropical I plead ignorance."

"It *is* something tropical," said Petrie. "It's *betel nut*."

Weymouth intruded quietly, and:

"Someone who chewed betel nut," he explained, "was hiding behind that sarcophagus lid when you brought Sir Lionel's body into this hut. Now, I'm prepared to hear that before that the door was unlocked?"

"You're right," I admitted; "it was. We locked it after his body had been placed here."

"As I thought."

Weymouth paused; then:

"Someone who chewed betel nut," he went on, "must have been listening outside Sir Lionel's tent when you decided to move his body to this hut. He anticipated you, concealed himself, and, at some suitable time later, with the key which Sir Lionel carried on his chain, he unlocked the door and removed the body!"

"I entirely agree," said Forester, staring very hard. "And I compliment you heartily. But—betel nut?"

"Perfectly simple," Petrie replied. "Many Dacoits chew betel nut."

At which moment, unexpectedly:

"Perhaps," came Rima's quiet voice, "I can show you the man!"

"What!" I exclaimed.

"I think I may have his photograph . . . and the photograph of *someone else!*"

3 TOMB OF THE BLACK APE

I MIGHT have thought, during that strange conference in the hut, that life had nothing more unexpected to offer me. Little I knew what Fate held in store. This was only the beginning. Dawn was close upon us. Yet before the sun came blushing over the Nile Valley I was destined to face stranger experiences.

I went with Rima from the hut to the tent. All our old sense of security was gone. No one knew what to expect now that the shadow of Fu Manchu had fallen upon us.

"Imagine a person tall, lean, and feline, high-shouldered, with a brow like Shakespeare and a face like Satan . . . long, magnetic eyes of the true cat-green . . ."

Petrie's description stuck in my memory; especially "tall, lean, and feline . . . eyes of the true cat-green . . ."

A lamp was lighted in Rima's tent, and she hastily collected some of her photographic gear and rejoined me as Ali came up shouldering his rifle.

"Anything to report, Ali Mahmoud?"

"Nothing, Effendim."

When we got back to the hut I could see how eagerly we were awaited. A delicious shyness which I loved—for few girls are shy—descended upon Rima when she realized how we were all awaiting what she had to say. She was so charmingly petite, so vividly alive, that the deep note which came into her voice in moments of earnestness had seemed, when I heard it first, alien to her real personality. Her steady gray eyes, though, belonged to the real Rima—the shy Rima.

"Please don't expect too much of me," she said, glancing round quickly. "But I think perhaps I may be able to help. I wasn't really qualified for my job here, but . . . Uncle Lionel was awfully kind; and I wanted to come. Really all I've done is wild-life photography—before, I mean."

She bent and opened a paper folder which she had put on the table; then:

"I used to lay traps," she went on, "for all sorts of birds and animals."

"What do you mean by 'traps,' Miss Barton?" Weymouth asked.

"Oh, perhaps you don't know. Well, there's a bait—and the bait is attached to the trigger of the camera."

"Perfectly clear. You need not explain further."

"For night things, it's more complicated; because the act of taking the bait has to touch off a charge of flash powder as well as expose the film. It doesn't work very often. But I had set a trap—with the camera most cunningly concealed—on the plateau just by the entrance to the old shaft."

"Lafleur's Shaft!" I exclaimed.

"Yes. There was a track there which I thought might mean jackal—and I have never got a close-up of a jackal. The night before I went to Luxor something fell into my trap! I was rather puzzled, because the bait didn't seem to have been touched. It looked as though someone might have stumbled over it. But I never imagined that anyone would pass that way at night—or at any other time, really."

She stopped, looking at Weymouth. Then:

"I took the film to Luxor," she said. "But I didn't develop it until to-day. When I saw what it was, I couldn't believe my eyes! I have made a print of it. Look!"

Rima laid a photographic print on the table and we all bent over it.

"To have touched off the trigger and yet got in focus," she said, "they must have been actually coming out of the shaft. I simply can't imagine why they left the camera undisturbed. Unless they failed to find it or the flash scared them!"

I stared dazedly at the print.

It represented three faces—one indistinguishably foggy, in semi-profile. That nearest to the camera was quite unmistakable. It was a photograph of the cross-eyed man who had followed me to Cairo!

This was startling enough. But the second face—that of someone directly behind him—literally defeated me. It was the face of a woman—wearing a black native veil but held aside so that her clear-cut features were reproduced sharply. . . .

Brilliant, indeterminably oblique eyes . . . a strictly chiselled nose, somewhat too large for classic beauty . . . full lips, slightly parted . . . a long oval contour. . . .

"That's a Dacoit!" came Petrie's voice. "Miss Barton, this is amazing! See the mark on his forehead!"

"I have seen it," Rima replied, "although I didn't know what it meant."

"But," I interrupted excitedly, as:

"Greville," Forester cried, "do you see!"

"I see very plainly," said I. "Weymouth—the woman in this photograph is *Madame Ingomar!*"

§ 2

"WHAT IS Lafleur's Shaft?" Weymouth asked. "And in what way is it connected with Lafleur's Tomb?"

"It isn't connected with it," I replied. "Lafleur's Tomb —also known as the Tomb of the Black Ape—was discovered, or rather suspected to exist, by the French Egyptologist Lafleur, about 1908. He accidentally unearthed a little votive chapel. All the fragments of offerings found were inscribed with the figure of what appeared to be a huge black ape—or perhaps an ape-man. There's been a lot of speculation about it. Certain authorities, notably Maspero, held the theory that some queer pet of an unknown Pharaoh had been given a freak burial.

"Lafleur cut a shaft into a long zigzag passage belonging to another burial chamber, which he thought would lead him to the Tomb of the Black Ape. It led nowhere. It was abandoned in 1909. Sir Lionel started from a different point altogether and seems to have hit on the right entrance."

"Ah!" said Weymouth. "Then my next step is clear."

"What is that?"

"I want you to take me down your excavation."

"Good enough," said I, "shall we start now?"

"I think it would be as well." He turned to Forester. "I want Greville to act as guide and I want you and Petrie to look after Miss Barton in our absence."

"We shall need Ali," I said, "to go ahead with lights."

"Very well. Will you please make the necessary arrangements?"

Accordingly I relieved Ali Mahmoud of his sentry duties and had the lanterns lighted. They were kept in the smaller hut. And presently Weymouth and I were on the ladders. . . .

The first part of our journey led us down a sheer pit of considerable depth. At the bottom it gave access to a sloping passage, the original entrance to which had defied all our efforts to discover it.

This was very commonplace to me, but I don't know how that first glimpse of the pit affected Weymouth. The night was black as pitch. Dawn was very near. Outlined by the light of the lanterns Ali carried, that ragged gap far below, to reach which we had been at work for many months, looked a likely enough portal to ghostly corridors.

An indescribable smell which characterizes the tombs of Upper Egypt crept up like a hot miasma. Our ladders were fairly permanent fixtures sloping down at easy gradients from platform to platform. The work had been fenced around; and, as we entered the doorway, watching the Arab descending from point to point and leaving a lantern at each stopping place, a sort of foreboding seemed to grab me by the throat.

It was unaccountable, or so I thought at the time, but it was well founded, as events were soon to show. I glanced at Weymouth. The big man was looking doubtfully at the ladders, but:

"It's safe enough," I said, "even for your weight. The chief is as heavy. I'll lead the way."

And so we set out, descending slowly. When at last the rubble-covered floor of the tunnel was beneath our feet, Weymouth paused, breathing deeply.

"That's the way to the original entrance," I said, pointing, "up the slope. But it's completely blocked fifteen yards along. There must be a bend, or a series of bends, because where it originally came out heaven only knows. However, this is our way."

I turned to where the shadowy figure of Ali waited, a lantern swinging in either hand so that the light shining up onto his bearded face lent it an unfamiliar and mask-like appearance. I nodded; and we began to descend the tunnelled winding slope. At a point just before we came to the last bend, Ali paused and held up one of the lanterns warningly.

"There's a pit just in front of us, Weymouth," I explained. "It doesn't lead anywhere but it's deep enough to break one's neck. Pass to the left."

We circled cautiously around the edge of this mysterious well, possibly designed as a trap for unwary tomb robbers. Then came the sharp bend, and here Ali left one of his two lanterns to light us on our return journey. The gradient became much steeper.

"We were starting on a stone portcullis which the chief believed to be that of the actual burial chamber," I explained, as we stumbled on downward in the wake of the dancing lantern. "He had a system of dealing with these formidable barriers which was all his own. Probably a few hours' work would have seen us through. Here we are!"

Ali paused, holding the lantern above his head. . . . And, as he did so he uttered a loud cry.

I pushed past Weymouth in the narrow passage and joined the headman. He turned to me in the lamplight. His face was ghastly.

"Good God!" I clutched the Arab's arm.

A triangular opening, large enough to admit a man, yawned in the bottom left-hand corner of the portcullis!

Ali raised his lantern higher. I looked up at a jagged hole in the right top corner. . . .

"What does this mean?" Weymouth demanded hoarsely.

"It means," I replied, in a voice as husky as his own, "that someone has finished the job . . . and finished it as Sir Lionel had planned!"

§3

THE TOMB of the Black Ape was extraordinary.

Whilst structurally it resembled in its main features others with which I was familiar, it was notable in its possession of an endless fresco of huge black apes. There were no inscriptions. The sagging portcullis, viewed from the interior of the chamber, created an odd hiatus in the otherwise unbroken march of the apes.

Low down in the corner of one wall was a square opening which I surmised must lead to an antechamber such as is sometimes found. The place contained absolutely nothing so far as I could see except a stone sarcophagus, the heavy lid of which had been removed and laid upon the floor. Within was a perfectly plain wooden mummy case, apparently of sycamore, its lid in position.

I was defeated. Either the mummy case was the least valuable object in the burial chamber, and everything else had been looted, or the thieves had been interrupted in the very hour of their triumph!

I hope I have made the scene clear, Ali standing almost as still as a statue, holding his lantern aloft; Weymouth a dim figure at one end of the sarcophagus, and I facing him from the other; the black apes marching eternally around us. Because this was the scene, deep there in the Egyptian rock, upon which eerily a *sound* intruded. . . .

"What's that?" Weymouth whispered.

We stood listening, reduced to that frame of mind which makes sane men believe in ghosts.

And, as we listened, the sound grew nearer.

It was made by soft footsteps. . . .

Weymouth recovered himself first; and:

"Quick," he whispered to Ali, "through the opening!"

He pointed to that square gap which I have mentioned and which I supposed to communicate with an antechamber.

"Quiet!" he added. "Not a sound!"

Led by Ali, we crossed the chamber, and as the headman stooped and disappeared only a dim and ghostly light shone out to guide us.

"Go on!" Weymouth urged.

I ducked and entered. Weymouth followed.

"Cover the lantern!"

Ali began to speak rapidly in Arabic, but:

"Cover the lantern!" Weymouth repeated angrily. "Be quiet!"

Ali threw something over the lantern and we found ourselves in utter darkness.

In a low tone, the headman began to speak again, but:

"Silence!" Weymouth ordered.

Ali Mahmoud became silent. He was one of the bravest men I have ever known, but now his broken tones spoke of fear. Partially, I had gathered what he wanted to say. My recognition only added to the horror of the situation.

That quiet shuffling had ceased. The air was indescribably stuffy, as one finds in such places. I knelt, resting my shoulder against the side of the opening, hoping that I might have some view of the outer chamber if anyone carrying a light should enter it.

Hard breathing in my ear told of Weymouth's nearness.

Of the size or shape of the place in which we were hiding I had formed no impression whatever.

Then, they began to advance again . . . soft footsteps.

"Whoever comes," Weymouth whispered, "don't stir!"

There was absolute silence. I found myself listening to the ticking of my wrist watch. A minute passed.

Then dawned a dim light. It outlined the triangle beside the portcullis.

The light increased. I recognized it as the ray of an electric lamp. And in some strange way this discovery was a relief. I suppose, without recognizing the fact, I had been in the grip of superstitious fear. God knows *what* I had expected! But the approaching threat became less horrible at the moment I realized the presence of modern science in its equipment.

Weymouth's breathing had ceased to be audible.

A figure appeared in the opening. . . . a fan of white light spread itself across the floor.

The figure stooped and entered. . . . I saw an Arab woman robed in shapeless black, her pose furtive. She held a flash-lamp, casting its ray all about the burial chamber. This was anomaly enough. But I was less concerned with it than with the hand that held the torch. . . .

A delicately slender hand it was, nurtured in indolence —an unforgettable hand, delicious yet repellant, with pointed, varnished nails: a cultured hand possessing the long, square-jointed thumb of domination; a hand cruel for all its softness as the velvet paw of a tigress.

My breath came sharply. Weymouth's fingers gripped my shoulder.

Had he seen what I had seen? Did he understand?

The woman crossed in the direction of the sarcophagus. I saw that she wore loose slippers—that her ankles were of that same dull ivory as the chaste, voluptuous hand.

She disappeared. Only by those shadows which the torchlight cast could I judge of her movements. She went all but silently in those soft slippers, but I thought that she had stooped to examine the sarcophagus. Apparently she made no attempt to raise its wooden lid. The light grew brighter—ever brighter.

She was approaching the low entrance to that antechamber in which we crouched!

At the very threshold she paused.

The light of her lamp painted a white fan which extended to within a few inches of my knees, touching nothing but rugged floor. By sheer chance—as I thought, then—no one of us came within its radius.

It moved, shining now directly upon the triangular opening beside the portcullis. I could see the woman's body as a dim outline. She stooped and went out. I listened to the rubble moving beneath her slippered feet as she mounted the sloping passage. Weymouth's breathing became audible again close to my ear. The sound receded . . . receded . . . and ceased; then:

"Quiet!" Weymouth whispered. "Don't move until I give the word."

My legs were aching because of the discomfort of my position, but I stuck to it, still listening intently.

Absolute silence. . . .

"Ali," Weymouth directed. "Uncover the light."

Ali Mahmoud dragging his robe from the lantern, dim yellow light showed us the low-roofed, rough-hewn chamber in which we crouched.

"Effendim!" Ali exclaimed, in quivering tones. "I saw him when first we came in. Look!"

Face downwards upon a mound of rubbish in an angle farthest from the entrance, was a brown man naked except for his loincloth and dark turban knotted tightly about his head!

"He is cold," Ali continued; "and as I knelt in the darkness I had to support my weight upon his dead body. . . ."

§ 4

ON HANDS and knees I crawled out into the passage. I contrived to make no sound.

I looked to my left.

Ali's lantern was just visible at the bend. Standing upright, I headed for it, stepping warily. At the corner I dropped to my knees again and stared up the slope. She was not in sight: I could trace the path beyond the wall to the next bend.

I proceeded. . . .

In view of the ladders I pulled up. A vague light, moon rays on black velvet, broke the darkness. I thought perhaps it came down the shaft . . . but it began to fade.

I hurried forward. I reached our excavation and looked up. No one was on the ladders.

Hopelessly puzzled I stood, listening.

And in that complete stillness I heard it again . . . the sound of footsteps softly receding. . . .

She had gone up the steep slope which led to the former entrance—but which now ended in an impassable mass of rock!

I had her!

Weymouth's instructions were forgotten. I meant to make a capture! This woman was the clue to the mystery. . . . It was she who had stolen the chief's body—and even without the clue provided by Rima's camera, I should have known her in spite of disguise.

Madame Ingomar!

Scrambling over irregular masses of stone, I had not gone five paces, I suppose, before a definite tact intruded itself. Whereas the air in the lower passage was fetid, almost unbreathable, here it was comparatively fresh.

I came to the angle, rounded it, and stopped. . . . I shot the ray of a torch ahead, expecting a wall of rock.

An irregular opening, some five feet high, yawned, cavernesque, right of the passage!

Running forward, I climbed through, throwing the ray of my torch before me. This opening had been completed at some earlier time, closed up and camouflaged.

I stood in a shallow pit. A ladder rested beside me, rearing its length into the darkness above. All this I saw as I stared upward, intently.

Light in hand, I mounted the ladder. . . . I found myself in a low tunnel. I stood still, listening, but could detect no sound. I pushed on, cautiously, the air growing ever fresher, until suddenly recognition came.

Switching off the light, I stared up to an opening where one pale star hung like a diamond pendant.

The passage ahead of me was empty. But I knew, now, where I stood, and I knew how the woman had escaped. . . .

This was *Lafleur's Shaft!*

§5

WEYMOUTH nodded, looking very grim.

"We are dealing with a she-devil," he said, "and I suppose she came to look for her servant."

He shone a light upon the upturned face of the man we had found in that chamber. It was a lined, leering face, hideous now by reason of the fact that the man had died from strangulation. Between the brows was a peculiar, coloured mark—how produced I could not imagine. But it appeared to have been seared in the yellow flesh, and then enamelled in some way.

"A Burman," Weymouth went on, "and a religious Dacoit."

He touched the mark with his finger, then stood still, listening. We all three listened, breathlessly—yet I dare swear no one of us knew what he expected to hear.

I thought as I looked down at those distorted features that if the slanting eyes were opened, this might well be a twin brother of the malignant creature who had followed me to Cairo.

"What does it all mean?" I asked.

"It means that our worst suspicions were correct," Weymouth replied. "If ever I saw one, this is a servant of Dr. Fu Manchu! This carries me back, Greville, to a scene in Sir Lionel's house late in 1913—the death of the Chinaman, Kwee. It may be a coincidence but it's an odd one. Because Kwee met his death when he was engaged on the same duty which I presume brought this yellow demon here."

"The murder of Barton?"

Weymouth nodded.

"Precisely. It's more than strange, and it's very horrible.'"

"Yet surely there's hope in it," I exclaimed excitedly. "This man belonged to the enemy. He has been strangled. It is just possible . . ."

"By heavens! it is!" he took me up. "After all he didn't die at the hands of his own friends."

"One thing is fairly certain," I said; "he came by the same route as the woman—by Lafleur's Shaft. What isn't certain is when a way was forced through."

"Nor *why* a way was forced through," Weymouth added. "What in heaven's name were they after? Is it possible"—he lowered his voice, staring at the procession of hideous, giant apes which marched eternally round the walls of the chamber—"that there was something in this tomb beyond . . ." He nodded in the direction of the sarcophagus.

"Quite possible," I replied, "but lacking special information to the contrary the first thing any excavator would do would be to open the mummy case."

"This seems to have been done."

"What!" I cried. "What!"

"Look for yourself," Weymouth invited, a curious expression in his voice.

He directed a ray on one end of the sarcophagus; whereupon:

"Good God!" I cried.

The wooden rivets had been removed, the lid raised and then replaced! Two wedges prevented its falling into its original position, leaving a gap of an inch or more all around. . . .

I stared in utter stupefaction, until:

"Have you any idea why that should be done?" Weymouth asked.

I shook my head. "Unless to make it easier to lift again," I suggested.

"If that was the idea," Weymouth went on quickly, "we will take advantage of it." He turned to Ali. "Hold the light—so. Now, Greville, get a grip with me, here. Don't move to any other part of the lid if you can avoid it—there may be fingerprints. And now . . . see if we can raise it."

In a state of such excitement as I cannot describe, I obeyed. Simultaneously we lifted, steadily. It responded to our efforts, being lighter than I had supposed. . . .

I fixed a half-fearful gaze upon its shadowy interior.

It appeared to contain a dull, gray mass, irregular in contour, provokingly familiar yet impossible to identify in that first dramatic moment. The very unexpectedness of its appearance destroyed my reasoning powers, temporarily defeating recognition.

When we had the lid at an angle of about forty-five:

"Hold it!" I called. "I'll take the other end."

"Right!" Weymouth agreed.

"Now!"

We lifted the lid bodily and laid it on the floor.

I could not have believed that that night of mystery and horror had one more thrill for my jaded nerves. Yet it was so, and it came to me then—an emotion topping all the others; such a thing as no sane man could have conjured up in his wildest imaginings. . . .

Amazed beyond reasonable articulation, I uttered a sort of strangled cry, staring—staring—down into the sarcophagus.

Overstrain and the insufferable atmosphere of the

place may have played their parts. But I must confess that the procession of apes began to move about me, the walls of the tomb to sway.

I became aware of a deadly sickness, as I stared and stared at the gray-white face of *Sir Lionel Barton*, lying in that ancient coffin wrapped in his army blanket!

PART TWO

4 *FAH LO SUEE*

"BETTER turn in, Greville," said Dr. Petrie rapidly. "Lie down at any rate. Can't expect you to sleep. But you've had enough for one night. *Your* job is finished for the moment. *Mine* begins."

How the others had reacted to our astounding discovery I am quite unable to relate. I was in no fit condition to judge.

Petrie half supported me along the sloping passage, and administered a fairly stiff peg from his flask which enabled me with Ali's aid to mount the ladders. I was furious with myself. To have to retire when the most amazing operation ever attempted by a surgeon was about to be performed—the restoring of a dead man to life! . . . But when at last I dropped down on my bed in the tent, I experienced a moment of horrible doubt—a moment during which I questioned my own sanity.

Ali Mahmoud's expression, as he stood watching me anxiously, held a certain reassurance, however. That imperturbable man was shaken to the depths of his being.

"Effendim," he whispered, "it is Black Magic! It is Forbidden this tomb!" He grasped an iron ring which he wore upon his right hand, and pronounced the *takbir*, being a devout Moslem. "Everyone has told me so. And it is true!"

"It would seem to be," I whispered. "Go back. You will be wanted."

I had always loved the chief, and that last glimpse of his gray-white face, under the astounding circumstances of our discovery, had utterly bowled me out. The things I had heard of Dr. Fu Manchu formed a sort of dizzy background—a moving panorama behind this incredible phantasy. There was no sanity in it all—no stable point upon which one could grasp.

Was Sir Lionel dead, or did he live? Dead or alive, who had stolen his body, and why? Most unanswerable query of all—with what possible object had he been concealed in the sarcophagus?

A thousand other questions, equally insane, presented themselves in a gibbering horde. I clutched my head and groaned. I heard a light footstep, looked up, and there was Rima standing in the opening of the tent.

"Shan, dear!" she cried, "you look awful! I don't wonder. I have heard what happened. And truly I can't believe it even now! Oh, Shan, do you really, really think—"

She fell on her knees beside me and grasped my hand.

"I don't know," I said, and scarcely knew my own voice. "I have had rather a thick time, dear, and I, well
. . . I nearly passed out. But I saw him."

"Do you think I could help?"

"I don't know," I replied wearily. "If so, Petrie will send for you. After all, we're quite in his hands. I don't want you to hope for too much, darling. This mysterious 'antidote' seems like sheer lunacy to me. Such things are clean outside the scope of ordinary human knowledge."

"Poor old boy," said Rima, and smoothed my hair caressingly.

Her touch was thrilling, yet soothing; and I resigned myself very gladly to those gentle fingers. There is nothing so healing as the magnetism of human sympathy. And after a while:

"I think a cigarette might be a good idea, Rima," I said. "I'm beginning to recover consciousness!"

She offered me one from a little enamelled case which I had bought in Cairo on the occasion of her last birthday—the only present I had ever given her. And we smoked for a while in that silence which is better than speech; then:

"I saw something queer," said Rima suddenly, "while you were away with Mr. Weymouth. Are you too weary —or do you want me to tell you?"

Her tone was peculiar, and:

"Yes—tell me what you saw," I replied, looking into her eyes.

"Well," she went on, "Captain Hunter came along after you had gone. Naturally, he was as restless as any of us. And after a while—leaving the hut door open, of course—I went and stood outside to see if there was any sign of your return. . . ."

She spoke with unwonted rapidity and I could see that in some way she had grown more agitated. Of course I had to allow for the dreadful suspense she was suffering.

"You know the path, at the back of the small hut," she continued, "which leads up to the plateau."

"The path to Lafleur's Shaft?"

Rima nodded.

"Well, I saw a woman—at least, it looked like a wo-man—walking very quickly across the top! She was just an outline against the sky, and I'm not positive about it at all. Besides, I only saw her for a moment. But I can't possibly have been dreaming, can I? What I won-dered, and what I've been wondering ever since is: What native woman—she looked like a native woman— would be up there at this time of night?"

She was sitting at my feet now, her arm resting on my knees. She looked up at me appealingly.

"What are you really thinking?" I asked.

"I'm thinking about that photograph!" she confessed. "I believe it was—Madame Ingomar! And, Shan, that woman terrifies me! I begged Uncle not to allow her to come here—and he just laughed at me! I don't know why he couldn't see it . . . but she is dreadfully evil! I have caught her watching you, when you didn't know, in a way . . ."

I bent down and rested my head against her tangled curls.

"Well?" I said, my arm about her shoulders.

"I thought you . . . found her attractive. Don't get mad. But I knew, I *knew*, Shan, that she was dangerous. She affects me in the same way as a snake. She has some uncanny power . . ."

"Irish colleens are superstitious," I whispered.

"They may be. But they are often wise as well. Some women, Shan—bad women—are witches."

"You're right, darling. And it was almost certainly Madame Ingomar that you saw!"

"Why do you say so?"

Then I told her what had happened in the tomb, and, when I had finished:

"Just as she disappeared," Rima said, "I heard foot-steps—quick, padding footsteps—on the other side of the wâdi. I called out to Dr. Petrie, but the sound had died away . . . I'd had one glimpse of him, though—a man running."

"Did you recognize him?"

"Yes."

Rima looked up at me reflectively, and:

"Do you remember an Arab who came into camp some days ago and insisted that he must see Uncle?"

I nodded.

"I think I know the man you mean—the chief asked me to find out what he wanted?"

"Yes."

"A gaunt-faced fellow—steely piercing eyes? Spoke very queer Arabic and denied all knowledge of English. Told me quite bluntly he had nothing whatever to say to *me*, but must see Sir Lionel. I finally told him to go to the devil. Why, good heavens, Rima . . . that was the evening before the tragedy!"

"Well," said Rima in a very low voice, "this was the man I saw running along the ridge to-night!"

"I don't like the sound of it," I admitted. "We have trouble enough already. Did he see you?"

"He couldn't have done. Besides, he was running at tremendous speed."

Even as she spoke the words, my heart seemed to miss a beat. I sprang up. Rima clutched me, her beautiful eyes widely opened.

Racing footsteps were approaching the tent!

I didn't know what to expect. My imagination was numb. But when the flap was dragged aside and Ali Mahmoud unceremoniously burst in, I was past reprimand, past any comment whatever.

"Effendim! Effendim! Quick, please. They tell me not to disturb Forester Effendim and Captain Hunter. . . . His camp bed!"

"What!—the chief's?"

"I am ordered to carry it up to the mouth of the old shaft!"

"Ali Mahmoud!"

Rima sprang forward and grasped the headman's shoulders.

"Yes! Yes!" His eyes were gleaming madly. "It is true, lady! It is Black Magic, but it is true."

Of all the queer episodes of that nightmare business there was none more grotesque, I think, than this of Ali and I carrying Sir Lionel's camp bed up the steep path to that gaunt and desolate expanse upon which Lafleur's Shaft opened. As we had come out of the chief's tent, I had heard the voices of Jameson Hunter and Forester in the big hut.

I was literally bathed in perspiration when we reached our goal. Dropping down upon the light bed, I stared out over that prospect beneath me. Right at my feet lay the Sacred Valley of Der-el-Bahari; to the right the rugged hills and ravines of this domain of the dead. Beyond, indicated by a green tracing under the stars, the Nile wound on like a river of eternity. For a few moments I regarded it all, and then Rima's fingers closed over my own.

A lantern stood at the mouth of Lafleur's Shaft.

We began to descend—to where a group awaited us.

Never, to the end of everything, shall I forget that moment when Weymouth and Dr. Petrie lifted Sir Lionel, still swathed in his worn army blanket, and laid him on the camp bed. Ali Mahmoud, who possessed the lean strength of a leopard, had carried him up the short ladder on his shoulders. But the effort had proved dangerously exhausting to the sufferer. Anxiety was written deeply upon Petrie's face as he bent over him.

Rima was almost as ghostly pale as he who had been plucked out of the gates of death. She was staring at Petrie fearfully, as one who glimpses a superman. But my own feelings were oddly compounded of joy and horror—joy because the dear old chief had been given a chance to live; horror, because I recognized a scientific miracle—and suddenly, awfully, appreciated the terrifying genius of Dr. Fu Manchu.

At which moment, Sir Lionel opened his eyes—gazed vacantly, and then saw us.

"Cheer up, Rima—child," he whispered. "God bless you fellows." And to me: "Thanks for the dash to Cairo. Good scout!"

He closed his eyes again.

§ 2

"WELL, NURSE," said Petrie, as Rima came out and joined us on the hotel terrace, "what do you think of our patient?"

Rima, a delicious picture in a dainty frock which had taken the place of the rough kit she wore in camp, fixed that grave look of hers on the speaker.

Then she turned swiftly aside, and I saw a threat of tears in her eyes.

"Yes," Petrie murmured. "I don't quite know what to make of him. I'm only an ordinary practitioner, Rima, and although I've searched every hotel in Luxor, this is an off-season. There isn't a man in Upper Egypt whose opinion I could take. And the only likely Cairo man, as bad luck would have it, is away on leave."

Silence fell between us. Sir Lionel Barton—first perhaps of modern Orientalists—lay in his room in a state of unconquerable coma, a mysterious secret locked in his memory. Petrie had rescued him from death—dragged him back, indeed, from the other side of that grim Valley—by virtue of an unnamed drug prepared by the greatest physician the world had ever known.

Strange, tragic, that so mighty a brain as that of Dr. Fu Manchu should be crooked—that an intellect so brilliant should be directed not to healing but to destruction. He was dead. Yet the evil of his genius lived after him. . . .

In a few weeks now this quiet spot in which we sat would be bustling with busy, international life. The tourist season would have set in. Dragomans, sellers of beads, of postcards and of scarabs would be thick as flies around the doors of the hotels. Thomas Cook's dahabîyehs would moor at the landing places; fashionable women would hurry here and there, apparently busy, actually idle: white-suited men, black-robed guides —bustle—excitement. . . .

Even now, as I stared across the nearly deserted roadway and beyond old peaceful Nile to where crags and furrows marked the last resting place of the Pharaohs, even now I could scarcely grasp the reality of it all.

What was the secret of the Tomb of the Black Ape? Careful examination had enabled us to prove that Lafleur at the time his excavation was abandoned—that is at the time of his disappearance in 1909—had got within a few yards of the passage leading to the burial chamber. Some unknown hand had completed the work and then had so carefully concealed the opening that later Egyptologists had overlooked it. Or had the hand been that of Lafleur himself?

More astounding still: the inner stone door, or portcullis, had been opened before! And it had been *reclosed* —so cunningly that even the chief had thought it to be intact! We were not the first party to reach it.

Therefore . . . when had the tomb been emptied? In Lafleur's time or a week ago whilst I was in Cairo? Who had reclosed it, and why had he done so? Above all—what had it contained?

Maddening to think that poor Sir Lionel might know . . . but was unable to tell us . . .

My musings were interrupted.

"Next to Brian Hawkins," came Petrie's voice, "of Wimpole Street, there's one man with whom I'd give half I possess to have ten minutes' conversation."

"Who is that?" Rima asked.

"Nayland Smith."

I looked across.

"Not as a professional consultant," Petrie added. "But somehow, in the old days, he seemed to find a way."

"Uncle was always talking about him," said Rima. "And I've hoped we should meet. He's chief of some department of Scotland Yard, isn't he?"

"Yes. He finally left Burma five years ago. And I'm looking forward to meeting him in England."

"Weymouth cabled him," said I, "but had no reply."

"I know." Petrie stared vacantly before him. "It's rather queer and quite unlike Smith."

"Is there really *nothing* we can do?" said Rima.

She rested her hand suddenly on Petrie's arm and I knew she feared that she might have offended him.

"I didn't mean you're not doing everything that's possible—I just mean do you think we're justified in waiting?"

"I don't!" he replied honestly; for honesty was the keynote of his character. "But I doubt if either of the men I mentioned could indicate any treatment other than that which we're following. Physically, Sir Lionel is gaining strength day by day, but his mental condition puzzles me."

"Is it contrary to your experience, Doctor," I asked; "I mean your experience of this strange drug which must have been used in his case?"

Petrie nodded.

"Quite contrary," he assured me. "The crowning triumph of Fu Manchu's method was their clean-cut effects. His poisons served their purpose to a nicety. His antidotes restored to normal."

A thick-set figure rounded the corner of the building and bore down upon us.

"Ah, Weymouth!" said Petrie. "You look as though a long drink with a lump of ice in it would fit the bill."

"It would!" Weymouth confessed, dropping into a cane chair.

He removed his hat and mopped his forehead.

"Any luck?" said I.

Whilst Petrie gave an order to a waiter, Weymouth shook his head sadly.

"Madame Ingomar is known to a number of people in Luxor and neighbourhood," he replied, "but not one of them can tell me where she lives!"

"It's therefore fairly obvious that she must have been either living in the native quarter or renting a villa!"

Weymouth looked at me with a tolerant smile, and:

"I agree," he replied. "My best local agent reported this morning, and you can take it for granted that madame has not been living in the native quarter. I have personally just returned from a very tiring inspection of a list of the available villas in and about Luxor. I can state with a fair amount of certainty that she did not occupy any of these."

A gentle rebuke which I accepted in silence. Dr. Petrie put the whole thing right, for:

"Scotland Yard methods have been pretty harshly criticised," said he, "generally by those who know nothing about them. But you must agree, Greville, that they don't fail in thoroughness."

He paused suddenly, arrested I suppose by my expression. I was staring at a tall Arab who, approaching the hotel, pulled up on sighting our group. His hesitation was momentary. He carried on, swung past us, and went in through the swing doors.

Rima sprang up and grasped my arm.

"The Arab," she cried, "the Arab who has just passed! It's the man I saw in camp. The man who ran along the top of the wâdi!"

I nodded grimly.

"Leave him to me!" I said, and, turning to Weymouth: "A clue at last!"

"Is this the mysterious Arab you spoke about?" excitedly.

"It is."

I dashed into the hotel. There was no sign of my man in the lobby, in which only vedettes of the tourist army, mostly American, were to be seen. I hurried across to the reception clerk. He knew me well, and:

"A tall Arab. Just come in," I said quickly. "Bedoui, Fargâni, or Maazâi, for a guess. Where's he gone?"

An assistant manager—Edel by name—suddenly appeared behind the clerk and I thought I saw him grip the latter's shoulder significantly; as:

"You were asking about an Arab who came in, Mr. Greville?" said he.

"I was."

"He is in the service of one of our guests—a gentleman of the Diplomatic Service."

"That doesn't alter the fact that he's been prowling about Sir Lionel's camp," I replied angrily. "There are one or two things I have to say to this Arab."

Edel became strangely embarrassed. His expression mystified me. He was Swiss and an excellent fellow; but reviewing what I had heard of the methods of Dr. Fu Manchu I began to wonder if my hitherto esteemed acquaintance might be a servant of that great and evil man!

"What's the name of this diplomat?" I asked rather shortly. "Do I know him?"

Edel hesitated for a moment; but at last:

"He is a Mr. Fletcher," he replied. "Please forgive me, my dear Greville, but I have orders in this matter."

Now definitely angry, but realizing that Edel wasn't to blame, I turned. Weymouth stood at my elbow.

"I respect your orders, Edel," I said, "but there can be no possible objection to my interviewing Mr. Fletcher's Arab servant?"

"May I add," said Weymouth harshly, "that I entirely agree with what Mr. Greville has said."

Edel recognized Weymouth; which seemed merely to add to his confusion of mind.

"If you will excuse me for a moment, gentlemen," he murmured, "I shall phone from the private office."

He withdrew—followed by the reception clerk, who obviously dreaded cross-examination.

I exchanged glances with Weymouth.

"What the devil is this all about?" he said.

There was an interval during which Dr. Petrie came in with Rima. At which moment Edel reappeared, and:

"If Mr. Greville and Dr. Petrie would be good enough to go up to Number 36," he requested, "Mr. Fletcher will be pleased to see them."

§ 3

"God knows we have trouble and enough," said Petrie, as the lift carried us to the third floor, "without the appearance of this unknown diplomat. I've never met a Mr. Fletcher. Can you imagine any reason why he should ask *me* to accompany you?"

"I can't," I admitted, and laughed, but not too mirthfully.

As we reached the third floor the Nubian lift-boy conducted us to the door of Number 36, pressed the bell, and returned to the lift.

The door opened suddenly. I saw a clean-shaven, thickset man, wearing a very well cut suit of the kind sometimes called "Palm Beach." With his black brows and heavy jaw, he more closely resembled a retired pugilist than any conception I might have formed of a diplomat.

Petrie stared at him in a very strange fashion; as:

"My name is Fletcher," he announced. "Dr. Petrie, I believe?" And then to me: "Mr. Greville? Please come in."

He held the door open and stepped aside. I exchanged glances with Petrie. We walked into the little lobby.

It was a small suite with a sitting room on the left.

Why did Mr. Fletcher open his own door when he employed an Arab servant?

I was gravely suspicious, for the thing was mysterious to a degree, but:

"Come right through!" cried a voice from the sitting room.

Whereupon, to add to my discomfort, Petrie suddenly grasped my arm with a grip which hurt. He stepped through the open doorway, I following close at his heels.

A window opened onto a balcony and to the right of this window stood a writing table. Seated at the table,

his back towards us, was the tall Arab whom we were
come to interview!

I noted with surprise that he had removed his turban,
and that the head revealed was not shaven, as I might
have anticipated, but covered with virile, wavy, iron-
gray hair.

Fletcher had disappeared.

As we entered, the man stood up and turned. The
deep brown color of his skin seemed in some way in-
congruous, now that he wore no turban. I noted again
the steely eyes which I remembered; the lean, eager
face—a face hard to forget once one had seen it.

But if I was perplexed, doubtful, my companion had
become temporarily paralyzed. I heard the quick intake
of his breath—turned . . . and saw him standing, a man
rigid with amazement, positively glaring at the figure
of the tall Arab beside the writing table!

At last, in a whisper, he spoke:

"*You!*" he said, "*you*, old man! Is this quite fair?"

The Arab sprang forward and grasped Petrie's hand.
Suddenly, seeing the expression in those gray eyes, I
felt an intruder. I wanted to look away; but:

"It isn't!" I heard; "and it hurts to hear you say it.
But there was no other way, Petrie. By heaven, it's good
to see you again, though!" . . .

He turned his searching glance upon me.

"Mr. Greville," he exclaimed, "forgive this comedy;
but there are vast issues at stake."

"Greville," said Petrie, continuing to stare at the
speaker with an expression almost of incredulity, "this
is Sir Denis Nayland Smith."

§ 4

"I FELT sure you would recognize Detective-Inspector
Fletcher," Nayland Smith declared. "You once spent a
night with him, Petrie—in the Joy Shop, down Limehouse way: Detective-Sergeant Fletcher he was then.
Have you placed him?"

Petrie's puzzled expression suddenly changed, and:

"Of course!" he cried. "I knew I'd seen him somewhere
—Fletcher! But what on earth is he doing *here?*"

"Ask what I'm doing here," snapped Nayland Smith. "One answer covers both questions. Fletcher's in my department of the Yard, now: you may remember he always specialized in Oriental cases. He's been posing as the principal, very successfully, whilst I, in the capacity of an Arab with whom he had confidential business, have been at liberty to get on with my job."

"But I don't understand," said I, "just what your job has been. I can't make out what a senior official of Scotland Yard is doing here in Luxor. It surely isn't usual? I mean, you've been hanging about our camp for some time past, sir.'"

Nayland Smith smiled; and—a magic of all rare smiles —my impression of his character was radically altered. I found myself for the first time at my ease with this grim Anglo-Indian. I saw behind the mask and I loved the man I saw.

"Damned *unusual*," he admitted, "but so are the circumstances." He turned to Petrie. "I didn't recognize Weymouth. I passed you very quickly. We must send for him. Fletcher can go."

He began to pace up and down the room, when:

"Smith!" Petrie exclaimed. "I don't understand. We're all in together. What had you to gain by this secrecy?"

Nayland Smith pulled up in front of him, staring down hard, and:

"Do you quite realize, Petrie," he asked, "with *whom* we're dealing?"

"No," Petrie replied, bluntly, "I don't."

Nayland Smith stared at him for a while longer and then turned to me.

"How much do you know of the facts, Mr. Greville?" he snapped.

"I have heard something of the history of Dr. Fu Manchu," I replied, "if that's what you mean! But Fu Manchu is dead."

"Possibly," he agreed, and began to walk up and down again—"quite possibly. But"—he turned to the doctor— "you recognize his methods, Petrie?"

"Undoubtedly. So did poor Barton! By sheer luck, as you know, I had a spot of the antidote. But whilst it has worked the old miracle, there are complications in this case."

"There are," said Smith. And stepping to the writing table he began to load a large and very charred briar with coarse-cut mixture from a tin. "It may be that the stuff has lost some of its potency in years—who knows? But one thing is certain, Petrie. I address you also, Mr. Greville."

He broke two matches in succession, so viciously did he attempt to strike them, but he succeeded with a third.

"All that fiendish armament is about to be loosed on the world again—perhaps reinforced, brought up to date. . . . And that's why I'm here."

Neither Petrie nor I made any comment. Nayland Smith, his pipe fuming between his teeth, resumed that restless promenade; and:

"You must know all the facts, Greville," he said rapidly. "Then we must form a plan of campaign. If only we can strike swiftly enough, the peril may be averted. It seems to be Fate, Petrie, but again I'm too late. Reports reached me from China, then from nearer home; from Cairo; from Moscow; from Paris and finally from London. Doubting everybody, I took personal action. And I definitely crossed swords with her for the first time at a popular supper restaurant in Coventry Street."

"Crossed swords with whom?" Petrie demanded, voicing a question which I myself had been about to ask.

But Nayland Smith, ignoring Petrie's question, continued to stride up and down, seemingly thinking aloud.

"New evidence respecting the sudden death of Professor Zeitland, the German Egyptologist, came to hand. I was satisfied that she was concerned. I sent Fletcher to interview her. . . .

"She had disappeared. We lost track of her for more than a week. All inquiries drew blank; until, by a great strike of luck, the French police identified her at Marseilles. She had sailed for Egypt.

"Good enough for me! I set out at once with Fletcher! Perhaps I shall be better understood if I say that the chief commissioner *sent* me. Since our one and only meeting, further advices from China had opened my eyes to the truth.

"I arrived in Port Said two weeks ago to-day. I had nothing to go upon—no evidence to justify summary action; only one fact and a theory. . . ."

His pipe went out. He paused to relight it.

"Do I understand, Sir Denis," I said, "that you're speaking of Madame Ingomar?"

He glanced at me over his shoulder.

"Madame Ingomar? Yes. That's a nom-de-guerre. Her dossier is filed at Scotland Yard under the name of Fah Lo Suee. You'll recognize her when you see her, Petrie!"

"What!"

"You met her once, some years ago. She was about seventeen in those days; she's under thirty, now—and the most dangerous woman living."

"But who is she?" cried Petrie.

Nayland Smith turned, a lighted match held between finger and thumb.

"*Dr. Fu Manchu's daughter,*" he replied.

5 NAYLAND SMITH EXPLAINS

"THE trail led me from Cairo to Luxor," said Nayland Smith. "Information with which I was supplied from day to day clearly pointed to some attempt on Sir Lionel Barton.

"Professor Zeitland, I had learned, from facts brought to light after his sudden and mysterious death, had been studying the problem presented to Egyptologists by Lafleur's Tomb, or the Tomb of the Black Ape. He had contemplated excavations. He deeply resented what he looked upon as Sir Lionel's intrusion. Did you know this?"

He turned to me suddenly. His skin, as I now realized,

had been artificially darkened. Looking out from that brown mask, his eyes were unnaturally piercing.

"Perfectly well."

Superintendent Weymouth, whose unexpected meeting with Sir Denis had reduced him to an astounded silence, now spoke for the first time since he had entered the room.

"Probably some of the professor's notes were stolen," he said.

"They were!" rapped Nayland Smith: "which brings us to Barton. Are his notes intact?"

He shot the question at me with startling rapidity.

"He made few notes," I replied. "He had a most astounding memory."

"In short, his memory was his notebook! This explains much. . . ."

He paused for a moment, and then:

"I immediately adopted the device which you know," he went on. "Fletcher installed himself here, and I used these rooms as my base of operations. I had first to track Fah Lo Suee to her lair. I use the term advisedly, for she is the most dangerous beast of prey which this century has known."

"I simply cannot understand," cried Petrie, "why Sir Lionel never suspected this woman!"

Nayland Smith shook his head irritably.

"I think he did—but too late. However—naturally I distrusted everybody, but I decided to take Barton into my confidence. It was on that occasion, Greville, that we met for the first time. I bear you no ill will, but I could have strangled you cheerfully. Short of revealing my identity, I was helpless . . . and I decided to stick to my disguise. . . ."

He shrugged his shoulders.

"I was wrong. The enemy struck. Forthright action might have saved him. I must have failed to do even what little I did do, for all the odds were against me, were it not that that very night I made up my mind to try to get to Sir Lionel secretly whilst the camp was sleeping.

"In one of your workmen, Greville—Said by name—I

recognized an old friend! Said was once my groom in Rangoon! I dug him out of his quarters at Kûrna and appointed him my liaison officer.

"Then, with Said in touch, I started. I had found one man I could trust. . . .

"I reached Barton's tent three minutes too late. He had just scrawled that last message——"

"What!" Weymouth interrupted excitedly. "You actually saw the message?"

"I read it," Nayland Smith replied quietly. "Barton, awakened by the needle, miraculously realized what had happened. I am prepared to learn that he expected it . . . that, at last, he had begun to distrust 'Madame Ingomar.' It had just dropped from his hand as I entered. "It was *my* voice, Greville, not his—that awakened you. . . ."

Nayland Smith ceased speaking, and stepping up to the table, began to knock ash from the steaming bowl of his briar, whilst I watched him in a sort of supefaction. Petrie and Weymouth were watching him too. Truly, here was a remarkable man.

"I slipped away as quietly as I had come. I watched for developments . . . then I set out for the head of the wâdi, where Said was watching. And Said had news for me. Someone had passed his hiding place ten minutes before—someone who slipped by rapidly. Said had not dared to follow. His orders were to wait . . . but I guessed that he had seen the agent of Fah Lo Suee who had entered Barton's tent ahead of me, and who had done his appointed work. . . .

" 'He was *Burmese*,' Said assured me, 'and I saw the mark of *kâli* on his brow!'

"In a deep hollow, by the light of my torch, I wrote a message to Fletcher. Said set out for Luxor. I was taking no chances. The result of that message, Petrie, you know—you also, Weymouth. Fletcher despatched two telegrams.

"Then I returned, and from the slope above Sir Lionel's tent, overheard the conference. I still distrusted everybody. As early as Lafleur's time, a certain person was interested in the Tomb of the Black Ape. Of this I am confident. The nature of his interest it remains for us to find out. In the meantime, a member of the family of that great but evil man has penetrated to the Tomb—"

"Smith!" Petrie interrupted. "Some age-old secret—probably a ghastly weapon of destruction—has lain there, for thousands of years!"

Nayland Smith stared hard at the speaker; then:

"Right," he snapped—"as regards the first part. Wrong as regards the second."

Giving us no chance to ask him what he meant:

"My point of vantage regained," he went on rapidly, "I saw all that took place. I saw the hut opened and two lanterns placed inside. I realized that it was proposed to carry Sir Lionel there. I saw the body placed in the hut, and the door locked. I could do no more—for Barton."

§ 2

"SINCE it seemed fairly certain that the objective of these mysterious crimes was the Tomb of the Black Ape, I now made my way round to the enclosure. The door was locked, but I managed to find a spot where I could climb up the fencing and look over. I stared down into the pit and listened intently. In that silence, any movement below must have been clearly audible. But I could not hear a sound.

"I was mystified—utterly mystified. I began to wonder if poor Barton had been mistaken in his own symptoms. I began to think he might really be dead! Perhaps the man whom Said had seen had had no connection with the matter. For I confess I could imagine no object in inducing that form of artificial catalepsy of which we know Dr. Fu Manchu to have been a master.

"Crawling above the camp like a jackal, I taxed my brain to discover some line of action.

"None of you slept much that night, and I had to watch my steps. It was a nerve-racking business, especially as I suspected that a trained assassin was prowling about somewhere—and possibly covering my movements.

"Failure seemed to threaten me again. I had failed in London. I had failed here. But I was expecting the return of Said at any moment, now, and presently I heard our prearranged signal: the howling of a dog.

"He, as least, had done his job. I replied.

"Perhaps my imitation was a poor one. All I know is that you, Greville, and others, came out into the wâdi with lanterns, and began to search all about the camp."

"We did," I interrupted. "That howling was unnatural. Dogs never came as near to the camp at such an hour."

"You found nothing," Nayland Smith went on; "and when all was quiet again, I crept round and rejoined Said. He had more news. As he had pulled across from Luxor to Kûrna, and in sight of the landing place, a motor-boat had passed, heading *upstream*. Note that, Weymouth. Standing in the bows was the Burman whom Said had seen near Sir Lionel's camp!

"This set me thinking. I came back here and turned up some recent reports. I discovered, Weymouth, that a certain Sheikh Ismail—who once slipped through our fingers in London—was living in the Oasis of Khârga. This venerable gentleman, for he must be well past eighty, I believe to be the present holder of the title of Sheikh al-Jébal, or head of the murderous sect of the *Hashishîn!*"

"A member of the old group!" said Weymouth excitedly.

"Exactly! And an associate of Dr. Fu Manchu! As a result, after a few hours' rest, I started for Esna. And I spent a very profitable day there."

"Esna!" I exclaimed. "Why Esna?"

"Because the old caravan road to the oasis starts from there, and because Esna is *upstream*. But whilst I was so employed, there's little doubt, I think, that Fah Lo Suee and her party, operating from Lafleur's Shaft, were completing the work begun by Barton. . . ."

"Amazing," I interrupted, "but fate, I suppose, that not a soul went down all day. The men, of course, were given a holiday."

"I know," Smith said. "Said was with *me*. However, I got back just before dusk and went straight to the camp to see how the land lay. Everything seemed to be quiet, and I was following the edge of the wâdi and had reached a point just above the hut in which Sir Lionel's body lay, when I pulled up . . . .

"It must have been inaudible from the tents. It came from directly below me—a soft, wailing cry. But I knew it! Good God, how well I knew it! . . .

"The call of a *dacoit!*

"Over these dangerous madmen, Greville, as well as the thugs and the hashishîn, the late Dr. Fu Manchu had acquired a mysterious control. I dropped flat on the ground, wriggled to the edge and looked down. Nothing moved—the place was dark and silent. But I continued to watch and presently I saw a seeming miracle.

"The door of the hut was open! I clenched my fists and stared. It was as though the gate of a tomb had opened. I did not know *what* to expect. But what I saw was this:

"A thickset brown man, naked except for his loincloth, came out, bending double in the manner of a laden Eastern porter, and carrying on his shoulders the body of Sir Lionel Barton wrapped in a gray blanket!

"On the threshold, he laid him down. He locked the door with a key he carried, shouldered the body again, and set off up the wâdi. . . . How had he got into the hut and where had he obtained the key?"

"Weymouth has solved that mystery," Petrie interrupted. "The key was on Sir Lionel's chain. He had only partially undressed on the previous night, and the Dacoit must have slipped in between the time that the hut was open and the time that Sir Lionel was carried there."

Nayland Smith tugged at his ear, a nervous mannerism which I had already observed, and turning to Weymouth:

"Congratulations!" he said. "What was your clue?"

"The man had been chewing betel nut. I found some . . ."

"*Chunam!* Brilliant, Weymouth! No school to equal that of experience. But do you grasp the astounding fact that he had stuck to his post for some *twenty hours*, with nothing but betel nut to sustain him! Yet he still had the strength of a tiger—as I was to learn! . . .

"I started to follow. By the smaller hut as you know,

Greville"—turning to me—"there's a steep path leading to the plateau: it begins as a sort of gully. And in the dense shadow there my Dacoit stopped.

"Need I say that I was searching madly for a proper course of action? What was the right course? Barton, if not dead, was palpably unconscious. What was the purpose of this mysterious body-snatching? Even if they knew that you, Petrie, had been sent for—"

"They did!" I interrupted. "I was followed to Cairo!"

"Even so, I argued, it must be as Barton himself had believed. Someone needed him—*alive!* My decision was made. I would not arouse the camp—my first, natural impulse—nor interfere in any way. I would follow and see where he was being taken.

"At which moment I nearly made a fatal mistake. I was on the point of moving from the deep belt of shadow in which I lay concealed, when a second soft call drew my gaze upward to where the path ceased to be a ravine and topped the slope above.

"Another Dacoit was descending, almost silently, but very swiftly.

"I shrank back.

"A low-toned conversation took place in the darkness beneath me; and then the pair raised the body of Sir Lionel and carried it rapidly up the slope and over the top.

"I gave them twenty seconds. I could risk no more. Then, fairly silent in my soft slippers, I raced up and threw myself prone on the crest. . . . They were heading westward across the plateau.

"Naturally, I had made myself acquainted with the outstanding peculiarities of the district immediately surrounding Sir Lionel's excavation; and in a flash, as I lay there, plainly visible in the moonlight should either of the Dacoits have looked back, the truth dawned upon me. I knew where they were making for.

"They were carrying him to Lafleur's Shaft!"

§ 3

"WHEN at last, using what little cover I could find, I ventured to approach the entrance to the shaft—which,

I discovered, is a long, sloping tunnel—the Dacoits were already far ahead of me. I could just see the moving light of a lantern.

"I stopped, lying flat by the entrance and looking down. What should I do next?

"For one moment the dreadful idea came to me that they were going to bury him—alive! I had it in mind to rush back to the camp for assistance, since I was single-handed and had no notion how many the enemy numbered.

"Wiser second thoughts prevailed. Sir Lionel lived. And they needed his *knowledge*. . . .

"Of Lafleur's Shaft I knew next to nothing. From what little I had gathered of its history, I understood that it was an abandoned cutting, terminating in a dead-end some forty feet below the level of the plateau.

"I waited—until I thought I might venture to descend the shaft to the first bend. It was hot and still—very still. No light showed ahead of me nor could I hear a sound. My sense of mystification increased. Where had they gone? What was their purpose?

"Risking everything, I flashed a light along the sloping path below me. I saw a rough tunnel terminating in another bend. I began to descend it. Sometimes my foot slipped and I stopped, listening. . . . Not a sound. I descended still further. Lafleur's Shaft, I learned, forms roughly a slanting figure Z. At last I came to a yawning pit. One fact my lamp revealed—the fact that a ladder rested in it. I stood in darkness, listening again.

"I could hear nothing.

"Using my lamp sparingly, I found my way to the head of the ladder and climbed down. On an irregular mass of stone at the base I paused. So far as my scanty information carried me, this was the end of Lafleur's Shaft. It was empty!

"Where had the Dacoits gone?

"I knew, from experience of these wiry little Burmans, that they possessed a gorilla-like strength and that for one to have carried even so heavy a man as Sir Lionel Barton down the ladder slung across his shoulders was not an impossible task.

"But where had they gone?

"Cautious examination discovered a ragged gap in one wall of the pit, or well, in which I stood. I groped my way through and found myself in a slanting passage running, roughly, parallel with the tail of the Z of Lafleur's Shaft, but hewn in the solid rock and obviously of very early origin.

"Far below to my right, a vague light showed. . . .

"I stood still again, listening.

"Voices . . . then a crashing, booming sound.

"I crept down the slope. I came to a second ladder, and looking up saw the stars. This was Barton's excavation! A dim perception of the truth began to dawn on me. I stole down a little further. I lay flat in the passage —watching.

"In the light of several lanterns I saw a party of half-naked men working feverishly to break away through the wall! They worked under a *woman's* direction! I heard her voice—an unforgettable, bell-like voice. . . ."

"Madame Ingomar!" I shouted—my pent-up excitement at last expressing itself.

"Undoubtedly Fah Lo Suee. She was questioning Barton, who lay in the passage . . . *and Barton was answering her!*"

§ 4

"BEYOND doubt they had been at their task for hours. Barton, unwillingly—perhaps unwittingly—helped them to complete it. They forced the opening. They all went through—four men led by Fah Lo Suee. Sir Lionel was left where he lay.

"I began to move back to the ladders. I had them in a trap! Not daring to use a light, I groped my way to the foot of the pit. I climbed to the first platform. Now, using my torch, I went up to the second.

"Switching off the torch, I pressed myself against the side of the excavation.

"Three lanterns passed the gap below. I counted them. Their bearers were heading for Lafleur's Shaft. There was an interval. Then, a fourth light shone out into the pit, it grew brighter.

"A woman, in native dress, looked up to where I crouched on the platform. . . .

"She withdrew, and went on. I heard a vague shuffling —a distant voice. Silence came. . . . Three men and one woman. Where was the *fourth* man—and Barton?

"The answer was all too obvious. . . . . Barton had served the purpose of Fah Lo Suee: his usefulness was ended. What ever she had sought, she had found. And now I realized that my immediate duty was to Sir Lionel. I crept down again, rung by rung. And, just as I reached the jagged opening, an explanation of the mystery of the fourth man burst upon me with icy certainty. . . .

"Already it might be too late! Barton had served the purpose for which he had been kept alive. Now, a *dead* man—not a synthetically dead man—he was to be re- placed in the hut. This was the task of the Dacoit who had carried him to Lafleur's Shaft, and who had re- mained behind to carry him back!

"A dim light shone through the newly made opening. I crawled nearer; so near that at last I could touch Sir Lionel's body.

"The Dacoit came out, stooping and holding the lan- tern. He would have been an easy shot but I had decided against the use of firearms. The professional strangler never had a chance; because I'd got my thumb on his jugular and my knee between his lean thighs almost be- fore he suspected I was there. I had little compunction; but these people are queerly constituted. This fellow had sinews like iron wire and the strength of a tiger. Yet, when I removed my grip and wondered how I should tie him up . . . he was dead!

"Perspiration blinded me and I was shaking with my exertions. I stood there, the fallen lantern at my feet, looking down at those two ghastly companions—the one indisputably dead; the other, for all his rigour and gray- white face, alive for all I knew to the contrary. Certainly, I had heard his voice not long since. . . .

"Taking up the lantern, which had remained alight, I stooped and went in through the triangular opening which had been made in the wall. . . . I found myself in the Tomb of the Black Ape!

"I need not describe it. The great sarcophagus was open—the wooden lid roughly in place, the stone one lying on the floor. I raised the sycamore covering. The mummy case was empty.

"Observing in a corner a cavern-like opening, I crossed and explored it. It proved to be a low antechamber. Into this I dragged the Dacoit so that he should be out of my sight. Then, I stood in the tomb, endeavouring to make up my mind what I should do about Barton.

"My brain was not at its best. But nevertheless I had to imagine what would happen when the Dacoit failed to report. Also, I had to take it for granted that my theory respecting his orders was correct; namely that his job was to carry Barton back to the hut, relock the door, and rejoin Fah Lo Suee wherever she might be.

"Suppose one of the enemy returned in my absence and found Barton where he lay? It was a dreadful possibility.

"First I thought of dragging him into the antechamber with the dead Dacoit. Then I realized that this would be useless. My second idea, wild though it sounds, was a good one. They would never think of looking in the *sarcophagus!* . . .

"The task was a heavy one. But I managed it. I replaced the lid, using some wedges which I found inside to prevent it closing entirely and to allow of air reaching the interior.

"I came out of Lafleur's Shaft. I heard the sound of a descending plane! At first, I couldn't believe my ears. Then came the explanation.

"And just as I grasped the fact that help for poor Barton—if he had not passed beyond its reach—was arrived, I heard a second sound . . . Said's signal!

"Appreciating his state of anxiety—I had been missing for hours—I circled round the camp and joined him. He had heard the descent of the plane, of course, but he was even more urgently concerned about a party of three men and a woman, the men bearing heavy burdens, who at that very moment, I gathered, were setting out on camels for Kûrna!

"I weighed the chances—and the stakes. I came to a

speedy decision. Leaving Said on duty, I set out for a point on the Kûrna road—where Fletcher was posted. . . .

"Needless to add, I failed to overtake Fah Lo Suee. Fletcher had noted the mysterious caravan, but naturally had not challenged it. I returned, and made my return known to Said. . . ."

"You alarmed the whole camp!" I broke in. "We had learned to recognize that false dog's howling!"

"Quite!" Nayland Smith smiled his rare, revealing smile. "But Said informed me that Rima Barton, who had been here, in Luxor, was back in camp with Ali Mahmoud and that you three fellows were with Forester in the big hut. . . .

"Dead beat though I was, another job remained: to enable you to find Barton! I sent Said out scouting. The last thing I desired was to make a dramatic entrance that night. Said presently returned to report that you, Weymouth, and Greville had gone to the excavation with Ali Mahmoud.

"I ordered Said to creep down Lafleur's Shaft and watch. . . .

"He was back in less than seven minutes by my watch! He had met a *woman* coming out! He thought that she had not seen him. She had gone towards the Valley. . . .

"My fatigue forgotten, I set out racing along the top of the wâdi—"

"Rima saw you!" I interrupted.

"Very likely. I observed that the door of the hut was open. . . .

"A wild-goose chase! Madame had vanished! With characteristic cool courage she must have returned to find out what had become of her missing servant.

"When the news reached me that Barton lived, I was worse than dog-tired; I was exhausted. And that night I shared a humble shakedown with Said."

§ 5

"I DISLIKE dividing our forces at this stage of the campaign," said Nayland Smith, "but there's nothing else for it. I had intended to send a message down, Petrie, if you hadn't anticipated me. As a matter of fact"—he glanced at the table—"I was writing it when the manager rang me up. I can play my lone hand no longer.

"Fletcher must stay on guard. We can't leave Sir Lionel unprotected. Rima, of course, must remain also. Indeed it would be useless to ask her to do otherwise. And I want you, Greville, to act as guide. It's a pretty desperate expedition. But there's a chance we may be able to strike quickly and strangle this dreadful business at the hour of its birth."

"Just a moment, Sir Denis," Weymouth interrupted. "Where do *I* come in?"

Smith turned to him, and:

"Glad to have you with me," he replied, "although your actual duty doesn't call for it."

"Thanks," said Weymouth dryly.

Smith met Dr. Petrie's fixed stare.

"Your leave starts next Thursday," he said. "And I can imagine how Karamanèh is looking forward to seeing London again. . . ."

There was a short silence, then:

"Is that all you have to say?" asked the doctor.

Nayland Smith grasped his shoulders impulsively.

"We stuck together pretty closely in the old days," he said. "But, now, I daren't ask you—"

"You don't have to!" Petrie declared truculently. "I'm coming!"

"But where are we for?" I asked.

"For the house at present occupied by Fah Lo Suee."

"What!" Petrie exclaimed. "Then where *is* this house?"

"Near the Oasis of Khârga—which accounts for Weymouth's inability to trace it!"

"But Khârga's surely a hundred and fifty miles!"

"There's a sort of railway," I said, "and a train about twice a year, from somewhere down Farshût way."

"Not our route," snapped Nayland Smith. "We're going from Esna."

"But that's just a caravan road—and a bad one too. The chief and I went, once—he had an idea of working on the Temple of Hibis there—and I'm not likely to forget it! Sir Lionel loves camels—and so we went on camels. It took us three days to get to Khârga and three days to get back!"

"What I wanted to know! We're going by car."

"Gad! There are some nasty bits!"

"There may be. But if Fah Lo Suee can do it, we can do it! The only car I could beg, borrow, or steal was a hard-bitten Buick about six years old. But I've got it packed in a quiet spot. I completed arrangements this morning. You might glance over this map."

From the table drawer he produced a large-scale map, when:

"What on earth are we going for?" Weymouth demanded.

"We're going to *spy!* To-night, I have reason to believe, the powers of hell will be assembled in el-Khârga."

§6

I WENT along to the room occupied by the chief, quietly opened the door, and looked in. He lay as I had last seen him, haggard, and pale under his tan. But his expression remained untroubled, and his strong, bronzed hands, crossed, rested quietly on the sheet.

Rima was sitting by the open window, reading. She looked up as I entered, shook her head and smiled rather sadly.

I went across to her.

"No change, dear?"

"Not the slightest. But you look excited, Shan. What is it? Something that extraordinary man Nayland Smith has told you?"

"Yes, darling. He has discovered what we wanted to know. We start in an hour."

Rima grasped my arm. Her eyes opened widely and her expression grew troubled; then:

"Do you mean—*her?*"

I nodded.

"Where she *is?*"

"Yes."

"Oh, that woman terrifies me! . . . I hate the thought of your going."

I put my arm around her shoulders.

"You have none of your old doubts, darling, have you?" I asked.

She shook her head, then nestled against me.

"But I'm afraid of her," she explained—"desperately afraid of her. She is evil—utterly evil. Where is this place?"

"In the Oasis of Khârga."

"What! But that's miles and miles away in the desert! How ever are you going to get there?"

I briefly explained Nayland Smith's plan; and when Rima understood that he as well as Weymouth and Petrie were coming with the party, she seemed to grow easier in mind. Nevertheless, I could see that she was very troubled. And I have often wondered since if some moment of prevision came to her—if she foresaw, dimly, that a dreadful danger lay awaiting me in the Oasis of Khârga. . . .

"To-night . . . the powers of hell will be assembled. . . ."

Nayland Smith's strange words recurred to me.

A sound of footsteps on the gravel in the garden below brought my mind sharply to present dangers. I crossed the balcony and looked down. One glance was sufficient to reassure me. Of course, I might have known!

Fletcher, pipe in mouth, was slowly pacing up and down—a sure guard, if ever a man had one.

"He stays there all the time, until the windows are closed," Rima explained. "Then he comes up and remains in the corridor."

I stooped for a moment over the chief, wondering what secrets were locked up in that big brain of his; wondering what had really happened down there in the Tomb of the Black Ape, and how much he knew regarding the missing contents of the sarcophagus. Rima stood beside me, and:

"You must be dreadfully tired, dear," I said.

"Oh, I get plenty of sleep," she replied, "in little bits. Nurse and I watch, turn and turn about, you know. I shouldn't be happy if I weren't doing it."

She looked up at me in that grave way which always made me ashamed of myself, made me feel that in some spiritual sense I was infinitely less than she. She lifted her lips to mine and I took her in my arms. . . .

Having little enough to do in the way of preparation, I might not have torn myself away so quickly had it not been for the arrival of the nurse, a stout and capable Scottish woman, well-known to the management.

Perhaps it was as well. Rima clung to me almost pitifully. . . . Yes! I think some Celtic premonition must have warned her. . . .

Downstairs I found Petrie waiting. Nayland Smith had disappeared; but:

"We are to join him at Esna," Petrie explained, "and for some reason which I should regard as lunatic in any other than Smith, we are to pose as natives!"

"What!"

"Complete outfits—of which he has quite a wardrobe —are ready in his rooms. Weymouth is up there, now . . . and Said is standing by to guide us to the meeting place."

We stared hard at one another. But neither of us was in jesting mood; and:

"Please God we all get back safe," said Petrie simply.

6 THE COUNCIL OF SEVEN

THAT journey across the desert was strange in many ways —stranger and more horrible in its outcome than a merciful Providence allowed me to foresee. Nevertheless it aroused within me that sort of warning sixth sense which once before, on the train to Cairo, had advised me of the fact that I was spied upon. Possibly those religious fanatics guarding the extraordinary woman who called herself Madame Ingomar, and whom I knew claimed a sort of divine ordinance for their ghastly crimes, reacted upon me in some odd way. All I know is that I seemed to have developed a capacity for smelling them out; as will presently appear.

Weymouth, Petrie, and Nayland Smith rode in the back of the car, and I sat in front with Said. The starting place outside Esna had been cunningly chosen and we had every reason to believe that the outset of our journey had been managed without attracting attention.

Our disguises were passably good. Both Weymouth and Petrie were well sun-browned, and I had the complexion which comes with months of exposure to the weather. Petrie's distinguished appearance was enhanced by a tarboosh and we had agreed to address him as "Bey." Weymouth, his robes crowned by a small white turban, resembled a substantial village sheikh; and I knew I could pass anywhere for a working Arab. Nayland Smith had retained the dress he was wearing at our first meeting.

Clear of the cultivated land that borders the Nile, and well out upon that ancient route which once had known no passage more violent than that of the soft padding camels and the tinkling of the camel bells, we met never a soul for thirty miles.

An hour, and another hour, we carried on, over desolate, gravelly, boundless waste. The sun blazed down mercilessly although it was dipping to the western horizon. On we went, and on; until, having mounted a long slope, I saw a wâdi ahead.

Nothing moved within my view, although I searched the prospect carefully through Nayland Smith's field-glasses. The ground was hard as nails. But at the bottom of this little valley, I spied a clump of palms and knew that there must be water.

A sentinel vulture floated high overhead.

We bumped on merrily across the wildest irregularities. In no sense was this a motor road. And, having carefully studied the map, I had serious doubts of its practicability beyond the site of some Roman ruins merely marked "el-Dêr."

Down we swept into the wâdi, Said driving in that carefree manner which characterizes the native chauffeur for whom tires are things made to be burst, and engines, *djinns* or powerful spirits invulnerable to damage. However, we carried three spares and could only hope for the best.

I don't know what it was, unless perhaps the smoother running of the car, which drew my attention to the path ahead. We were now in the cup of the valley and rapidly approaching that clump of palms which I had noted. Suddenly:

"Pull up," rapped Nayland Smith.

His hand gripped my shoulder. Said pulled up.

"Look!"

We all stood and stared ahead. Nayland Smith pointed. The surface was comparatively soft here; and clearly discernible upon the road, crossing and recrossing, were many tire marks!

"Fah Lo Suee!" said Smith, as if answering my unspoken query. "You can set your mind at rest, Greville. The road to Khârga is practicable for driving."

It was a curious discovery, and it set me thinking, hard. When Madame Ingomar had visited the camp, had she come all the way from the oasis, and had she returned there? Presumably, this was so. And, as always happened when my thoughts turned to this phenomenal woman, a very vivid mental picture presented itself before my mind. Her long, narrow, jade-green eyes seemed to be staring into mine. And I saw one of those small cigarettes which she loved, smouldering in a long engraved holder between delicate ivory fingers.

We passed the tree-shaded well, and mounted a stiff slope beyond. I cannot answer for the others, but, as I have indicated, my own thoughts were far away. It was just as we reached the crest, and saw a further prospect of boundless desert before us, that I became aware, or perhaps I should say conscious, of that old sense of espionage.

Nothing moved upon that desolate expanse, over which the air danced like running water. But a positive conviction seized me—a conviction that news of our journey had reached the enemy, or would shortly reach the enemy. I began to think about that solitary Pharaoh's Chicken—that sentinel vulture—floating high above the palms. . . .

"Stop!" I said.

"What is it?" snapped Nayland Smith.

"May be nothing," I replied, "but I want to walk back to the brow of the hill and take a good look at the wâdi through which we have just come."

"Good!" He nodded. "I should have thought of it myself."

I got out the glasses, slung them across my shoulder, and walked rapidly back. At a point which I remembered, because a great blackened boulder lying straight across the road had nearly brought us to grief, I stooped and went forward more slowly. This boulder, I reflected, might provide just the cover I required. Lying flat down beside the stone, to the great alarm of a number of lizards who fled rapidly to right and left, I focused my glasses upon the clump of trees below me.

At first I could see nothing unusual. But the vulture still floated in the sky and the significance of his presence had become unmistakable. . . . Some living thing was hidden in the grove!

Adjusting the sights to a nicety, I watched, I waited. And presently my patience was rewarded.

A figure came out of the clump of trees!

I could see him clearly and only hoped that he could not see me. He might have passed muster, except for his tightly knotted blue turban. Emphatically, he was not an Egyptian. Standing beside the irregularly marked path, he placed a box upon the ground. I studied his movements with growing wonderment.

What could he be about? He seemed to be fumbling in the box.

Then suddenly he withdrew his hand, raised it high above his head—and a gray pigeon swept low over the desert, rose up and up, higher and higher! It circled once, twice, three times. Then, straight as an arrow it set out . . . undoubtedly bound for the Oasis of Khârga!

§ 2

"VERY clever," said Nayland Smith grimly. "We shall therefore be expected. I might have guessed she wouldn't be taken unawares. But it confirms my theory."

"What theory?" Petrie asked.

"That to-night is a very special occasion at the house of the Sheikh Ismail!"

"We're running into a trap," said Weymouth. "Now that we know beyond any doubt that we're expected, what are our chances? It's true there's a railway to this place—but it's rarely used. The people of the oases have never been trustworthy—so that our nearest help will be a hundred and fifty miles off!"

Smith nodded. He got out and joined me where I stood beside the car, loading and lighting his pipe. He began to walk up and down, glancing alternately at me, at Weymouth, and at Dr. Petrie. I knew what he was thinking and I didn't interrupt him. He was wondering if he was justified in risking our lives on so desperate a venture; weighing the chances of what success might mean to the world against our chances of coming out of the job alive. Suddenly:

"What's the alternative?" he snapped, peering at Weymouth.

"There isn't one that I can think of."

"What do you say, Petrie?"

Petrie shrugged his shoulders.

"I hadn't foreseen this," he confessed. "But now that it's happened . . ."

He left the sentence unfinished.

"Get the map out, Greville," Nayland Smith rapped. . . . "Here, on the ground."

I dived into the front of the car and pulled out the big map. This we spread on the gravelly path, keeping it flat by placing stones on its corners. Weymouth and Petrie alighted; and the four of us bent over the map.

"Ah!" Nayland Smith exclaimed and rested his finger on a certain spot. "That's the danger area, isn't it, Greville? That's where we might crash?"

"We might!" I replied grimly. "It's a series of hairpin bends and sheer precipices, at some points fourteen hundred feet up. . . ."

"That's where they'll be waiting for us!" said Nayland Smith.

"Good God!" Petrie exclaimed.

I exchanged glances with Weymouth. The expression in his blue eyes was enigmatical.

"Do you agree with me?" rapped Smith.

"Entirely."

"In short, gentlemen," he went on, "if we pursue our present route it's certain we shall never reach el-Khârga."

There was an interval of silence; then:

"We might easily break down before we get to the hills," I said slowly. "No one at the other end would be the wiser, except that we should never enter the danger zone. Now"—I bent and moved my finger over the map—"at this point as you see, the old caravan road from Dongola to Egypt is only about thirty miles off. It's the Path of the Forty, formerly used by slave caravans from Central Africa. If we could find our way across to it, we might approach Khârga from the south, below the village marked Bûlag—it means a détour of forty or fifty miles, even if we can do it. But . . ."

Nayland Smith clapped me on the shoulder.

"You've solved the problem, Greville!" he said. "Nothing like knowledge of the geography of a district when one's in difficulties. We're in luck if we make it before dusk. But how shall we recognize the Path of the Forty?"

"By the bleached bones," I replied.

§3

SUNSET dropped its thousand veils over the desert. The hills and wâdis of its desolate expanse passed from a glow of gold through innumerable phases of red. We saw crags that looked yellow under a sky of green: we saw a violet desert across which the ancient route of the slave traders stretched like a long-healed scar. There were moments when all the visible world resembled the heart of a tulip. But at last came true dusk with those scattered battalions of stars set like pearls in a deep, velvet-lined casket.

Wonderful to relate, we had forced the groaning Buick over trackless miles southwest of the road, had found a path through the hills and had struck the Darfûr caravan route some twenty miles below el-Khârga. A difference in the quality of the landscape, a freshening and a cleanness in the air, spoke of the near oasis. Then, on a gentle slope:

"A light ahead!" Weymouth cried.

I checked Said. We all stood up and looked.

"That must be Bûlag," said Nayland Smith. "The house of the sheikh lies somewhere between there and el-Khârga."

"It's a straight road now," Petrie broke in. "Thank heaven, there's plenty of light. I'm all for blazing through the village as hard as we can go and then finding some parking place outside the town."

"Pray heaven the old bus can stand it!" Weymouth murmured devoutly.

And so, headed north, we set out. The road was abominable, but fairly wide where it traversed the village. Nayland Smith had relieved Said at the wheel and the scene as he coaxed a way through that miniature bazaar was one I can never forget. Every man, woman, child, and dog had turned out. . . .

"They may send the news to el-Khârga," said Smith, as we finally shook off the last pair of staring-eyed Arab boys who ran after us, "but we've got to chance it."

We parked the doughty Buick in a grove of date-palms just south of the town. Weymouth seemed to anticipate trouble with Said, but I knew the man and had never doubted that he would consent to stand by. We left him a charged repeater and spare shells, and there were ample rations aboard to sustain him during the time he might have to mount guard. We marked an hour on the clock when, failing our reappearance, he was to push on with all possible speed to the post office at el-Khârga and communicate with Fletcher. How he carried out these orders will appear later.

As the four of us walked from the palm grove:

"It's a good many years," said Weymouth, "since I disguised myself!"

I looked at him in the moonlight, and I thought that he made a satisfactory and most impressive sheikh. True, his Arabic was bad, but so far as his appearance went, he was above criticism. Dr. Petrie was a safe bet; and Sir Denis, as I knew, could have walked about Mecca unchallenged. For my own part I felt fairly confident, for I knew the ways of the desert Arabs well enough to be capable of passing for one.

"We may be too late," said Nayland Smith; "but I feel disposed, Greville, to make straight for the town; otherwise we might lose ourselves. Then, you acting as spokesman, since you speak the best Arabic, we can inquire our direction boldly."

"I agree," said I.

And so it was settled.

§4

EL-KHÂRGA, as I vaguely remembered, though a considerable town of some seven or eight thousand inhabitants, consisted largely of a sort of maze of narrow streets roofed over with palm trunks so as to resemble tunnels at night. We penetrated, and presently found our way to the centre of the place. A mosque and two public buildings attracted my attention; and:

"Down here," I said, "there's a café, where we shall learn all we want to know."

Two minutes later we were grouped around a table in a smoke-laden room.

"Look about," said Nayland Smith. "Kismet is with us. Whatever is going on in el-Khârga is being discussed here, to-night."

"I told you this was the place," said I.

But I looked about as he had directed. Certainly we had discovered the one and only house of entertainment in el-Khârga. . . . Little did I realize, as I considered our neighbours, where my next awakening would be!

Here were obvious townspeople, prosperous date-merchants, rice growers, petty officials and others, smoking their pipes in evening contentment. A definite odour of *hashîsh* pervaded the café. But the scene looked typical enough, until:

"Those fellows in the corner don't seem quite in the picture," said Weymouth.

I followed the direction of his glance. Two men were bending over a little round table. They smoked cigarettes, and a pot of coffee stood between them. In type, they were unfamiliar; unfamiliar in the sense that one didn't expect to come across them in an outpost of Egypt. In Cairo, they might have passed unnoticed, but their presence in el-Khârga was extraordinary. I turned to Nayland Smith, who was glancing in the same direction; and:

"What are they?" I asked.

"Afghans," he replied. "The great brotherhood of Kâli is well represented there."

"Remarkable," I said. "There can be few relations between Afghanistan and this obscure spot."

"None whatever!" Weymouth broke in. "And now, Greville, follow the direction in which my cigarette is pointing."

Endeavouring not to betray myself, I did as he suggested.

"A group of three," he added for my guidance.

I saw the group. I might have failed to identify them, but my memory was painfully fresh in regard to that dead man in the Tomb of the Black Ape. They wore their turbans in such a manner that the mark on the brow could not be distinguished. But I knew them for Burmans; and I did not doubt that they belonged to the mysterious fraternity of the Dacoits! At which moment:

"Don't turn around until I give the signal," Nayland Smith rapped—"but just behind us."

I watched him as he glanced about, apparently in search of a waiter, then caught his signal. I looked swiftly into an alcove under the stairs . . . and then turned aside, as the gaze of a pair of fierce, wild-animal eyes became focused upon mine. The waiter arrived and Nayland Smith ordered more coffee. As the man departed to execute the order:

"*Thugs!*" he whispered. He bent over the table. "There are representatives of at least three religious fanatical sects in this place to-night. *Dacoity* is represented, also *Thugee*. The two gentlemen from Kandahar are *phansigars*, or religious stranglers!" He stared at Weymouth. "Does this suggest anything to you?"

Weymouth's blue eyes were fixed on me; and:

"I confess, Greville," he said, "that I feel as you do. ... And I can see that you're puzzled."

"I am," I agreed.

Nayland Smith raised his hand irritably and tugged at the lobe of his left ear; then:

"*You* understand, Petrie?" he jerked.

I looked at Dr. Petrie and it was unnecessary for him to reply. I saw that he *did* understand.

"Any doubt I may have had, Smith," he said, "regarding the purpose of this expedition, is washed out. In some miraculous way you have brought us to what seems to be the focus of all the dangerous fanatics of the Eastern world!"

"I don't claim all the credit," Smith replied; "but I admit that the facts confirm my theory."

"And what was your theory?" I asked.

"My theory," Smith replied, "based on the latest information to hand, and, as Weymouth here knows, almost hourly reports from police headquarters as widely divided as Pekin and Berlin, was this: That some attempt was being made to coördinate the dangerous religious sects of the East together with their sympathizers in the West. In short that the organization once known as the *Si Fan*—you, alone, Greville," he turned to me, "fail to appreciate the significance of this—is in process of reconstruction! Something vital to the scheme was hidden in the Tomb of the Black Ape. This—and I can only blame myself—was removed under my very nose. The centre of the conspiracy is Fah Lo Suee—Dr. Fu Manchu's daughter, whose temporary headquarters I know to be here. To-night, at least, I am justified. Look around."

He bent over the table and we all did likewise, so that our four heads came very closely together; then:

"We are not too late," he said earnestly. "A meeting has been called . . . and we must be present!"

§ 5

THE TWO Indians in the alcove stood up and went towards the door. As the pair disappeared:

"They lead, and we follow!" said Nayland Smith. "Go ahead, Weymouth, and act as connecting link."

He stood up, clapping his hands for the waiter. Weymouth had his meaning in a moment, nodded, and went out.

"Follow him, Greville!"

I grasped the scheme and went out behind the superintendent. The spirit of the thing was beginning to get me. Truly this was a desperate adventure . . . for the stakes were life or death!

We were dealing with savagely dangerous characters who were, moreover, expert assassins to a man. Possibly those we had actually identified in the café represented only a small proportion of the murderous fanatics assembled that night in el-Khârga. . . .

Weymouth led and I followed. I had grasped Nayland Smith's routine—and I knew that Petrie would be behind me. The score discharged, Smith would track Petrie.

I saw the bulky form of the superintendent at the far side of the square. By a narrow street he paused, peered ahead, and then glanced back.

I raised my hand. Weymouth disappeared.

Reaching the street in turn, I looked along it. I saw a sheer tunnel, but recognized it for that by which we had reached the square. There was an open space at the further end; and I saw Weymouth standing there in the moonlight and knew that I must be visible to him—as a silhouette.

He raised his arm. I replied. Then I looked back.

Dr. Petrie was crossing the square!

We exchanged signals and I followed Weymouth. The chain was complete.

For a time I thought that the house of the Sheikh Ismail might be somewhere on the road we had pursued from the palm grove to the town. But it was not so. Weymouth, ahead of me, paused, and gave the signal: left.

A narrow path through rice fields, with scanty cover other than that of an occasional tree, proved to be the route. If the men walking a few hundred yards ahead of Weymouth looked around, they could scarcely fail to see him! I only prayed, should they do so, that they would take it for granted he was bound upon business similar to their own.

Where an acacia drooped over a dome, very white in the moonlight, which marked the resting place of some holy man, the path seemed to end. So also did the cultivated land. Beyond stretched the desert, away to the distant hills.

By the shrine Weymouth paused, turned, and signalled. I looked back. Petrie was not in sight. I waited, anxiously . . . and then I saw him, just entering the rice field.

We exchanged signs and I pressed on.

Left of the cultivated land, and invisible from the rice, was a close grove of dôm palms. As I cautiously circled around the shrine and saw nothing but desert before me, instinctively I looked to right and left. And there was Weymouth, not fifty yards away!

I joined him, and:

"The house is just beyond the trees," he said. "There's a high wall all around it. The two Indians have gone in."

We waited for Petrie. Then Nayland Smith joined us. He turned and stared back along the path. Evidently no other party was on the way yet. The track through the rice field was empty as far as the eye could see.

"What next?" said Smith. "I'm afraid I've left too much to chance. We should have visited the mudîr. The thing begins to crystallize. I know, now, what to expect."

He turned, and:

"Weymouth," he said, "do you remember the raid on the house in London in 1917?"

"By God!" cried Weymouth. "You mean the meeting of the Council of Seven?"

"Exactly!" Smith rapped.

"Probably the last."

"In England, certainly."

"The Council of Seven?" I said. "What is the Council of Seven?"

"It's the *Si Fan!*" Petrie replied, without adding to my information.

But the tone of his voice turned me cold in spite of the warmth of the night.

"The Council of Seven," Weymouth explained, in his kindly way, "was an organization with headquarters in China. . . ."

"In Honan," Smith jerked.

"The president, or so we always believed," Weymouth continued, "was Dr. Fu Manchu. Its objects we never learned except in a general way."

"World domination," Petrie suggested.

"Well, that's about it, I suppose. Their methods, Greville, included wholesale robbery and murder. Everybody in their path they removed. Poison was their favourite method, animal or vegetable, and they apparently controlled in their campaign the underworlds of Europe, Asia, Africa, and America. They made the mistake of meeting in London, and"—his tone grew very grim—"we got a few of them."

"But not all," Nayland Smith added. He suddenly grasped my shoulder, and: "Are you beginning to understand," he asked, "what was hidden in the Tomb of the Black Ape?"

I looked at him in blank surprise.

"I can see no connection," I confessed.

"Something," he went on tensely, "which has enabled the woman you know as Madame Ingomar after an interval of thirteen years, to summon the Council of Seven!"

§6

IN THE shadow cast by a lebbekh tree we all crouched, Nayland Smith having his glasses focused upon the door in a long high wall.

The two Afghans had approached and now stood before this door. So silent was the night that we distinctly heard one of them beat on the panels. He knocked *seven times*. . . .

I saw the door open. Faintly to my ears came the sound of a strange word. It was repeated—by another voice. The murderous Asiatics were admitted. The door was closed again.

"Representatives of at least two murder societies have arrived," said Smith, dropping the glasses and turning.

"We are learning something, but not enough. In short, how the devil are we going to get into that house?"

There was a pause and then:

"Personally," said Dr. Petrie, "I think it would be deliberate suicide to attempt to do so. We have not notified the officials of el-Khârga of our presence or our business; and as it would appear that the most dangerous criminal group in the world is assembling here to-night, what could we hope to do, and what would our chances be?"

"Sanity, Petrie, sanity!" Nayland Smith admitted. But the man's impatience, his over-brimming vitality, sounded in his quivering voice. "I've bungled this business—but how could I know? . . . I was guessing, largely."

He stood up and began to pace about in the shadow, carefully avoiding exposing himself to the light of the moon; then:

"Yes," he murmured. "We must establish contact with el-Khârga. Damnable!—because it means splitting the party. . . . Hello!"

A group of three appeared, moving like silhouettes against the high, mud-brick wall—for the moon was behind us. Nayland Smith dropped prone again and focused the glasses. . . .

"The Burmans," he reported. "*Dacoity* has arrived."

In tense silence we watched this second party receive admittance as the first had done. And now I recognized the word. It was *Si Fan!* . . . Again the great iron-studded door was closed.

"We don't know how many may be there already," said Petrie. "Possibly those people we saw in the café—"

"Silence!" Smith snapped.

As he spoke, a tall man dressed in European clothes but wearing no hat appeared around the corner of the wall and approached the door. He had a lithe, swinging carriage.

"This one comes alone," Nayland Smith murmured. He studied him through the glasses. "Unplaceable. But strangely like a Turk. . . ."

The tall man was admitted—and the iron-studded door closed once more.

Nayland Smith stood up again and began beating his fist into the palm of his hand, walking up and down in a state of tremendous excitement.

"We must *do* something!" he said in a low voice—"we must *do* something! Hell is going to be let loose on the world. To-night, we could nip this poisonous thing in the bud, if only . . ." he paused. Then: "Weymouth," he rapped, "you have official prestige. Go back to el-Khârga —make yourself known to the mudîr and force him to raise a sufficient body of men to surround this house! You can't go alone, therefore Dr. Petrie will go with you. . . ."

"But, Smith! . . ."

"My dear fellow,"—Nayland Smith's voice altered entirely—"there's no room for sentiment! We're not individuals to-night, but representatives of sanity opposed to a dreadful madness. Greville here has a peculiarly intimate knowledge of Arab life. He speaks the language better than any of us. This you will both admit. I must keep him by me, because my job may prove to be the harder. Off you go, Weymouth! I'm in charge. Get down the dip behind us and circle round the way we came. Don't lose a moment!"

There was some further argument between these old friends, but finally the dominating personality of Nayland Smith prevailed; and Weymouth and Dr. Petrie set out. As they disappeared into the hollow behind us:

"Heaven grant I haven't bungled this thing!" said Nayland Smith and gripped my arm fiercely. "But I've stage-managed it like an amateur. Only sheer luck can save us now!"

He turned aside and focused his glasses on the distant angle of the wall. A minute passed—two—three—four. Then came a sudden outcry, muffled, but unmistakable.

"My God!" Smith's voice was tragic. "They've run into another party! Come on, Greville!"

Breaking cover we hurried across in the moonlight. Regardless of any watcher who might be concealed behind that iron-studded door in the long wall, we raced headlong to the corner. I was hard and fit; but, amazing to relate, I had all I could do to keep pace with Nayland

Smith. He seemed to be a man who held not sluggish human blood but electricity in his veins.

Around the corner we plunged . . . and almost fell headlong over a vague tangle of struggling figures!

"Petrie!" Nayland Smith cried. "Are you there?"

"Yes, by the grace of God!" came pantingly. . . .

"Weymouth?"

"All clear!"

Dense shadow masked the combatants; and risking everything, I dragged out my torch and switched on the light.

Dr. Petrie, rather dishevelled and lacking his tarboosh, was just standing up. A forbidding figure, muffled in a shapeless camel-hair garment, lay near. Weymouth was resting his bulk upon a second.

"Light out!" snapped Nayland Smith.

I obeyed. Weymouth's voice came through the darkness.

"Do you remember, Sir Denis, that other meeting in London? There was only one Lama monk there. There are two here!"

His words explained a mystery which had baffled me. These were *Tibetan monks!*

"They must have heard us approaching," Petrie went on. "They were hiding in the shadows. And as we climbed up onto the path, they attacked us. I may add that they were men of their hands. Personally I'm by no means undamaged, but by sheer luck I managed to knock my man out."

"I think I've strangled mine!" said Weymouth grimly. "He was gouging my eye," he added.

"Petrie!" said Nayland Smith. "We're going to win! This is the hand of Providence!"

For one tense moment none of us grasped his meaning; then:

"By heavens, *no.* It's too damned dangerous," Weymouth exclaimed. "For God's sake don't risk it!"

"I'm going to risk it!" Smith snapped. "There's too much at stake to hesitate. If *they* were in our place, there'd be two swift executions. We can't stoop to that.

Gags we can improvise. But how the devil are we going to tie them up?"

At which moment the man on whose body Weymouth was kneeling uttered a loud cry. The cry ceased with significant suddenness; and:

"Two of us wear turbans," said Weymouth: "that's twelve feet of stout linen. What more do we want?"

We gagged and bound the sturdy Tibetans, using torchlight sparingly. One of them struggled a lot; but the other was still. Petrie seemed to have achieved a classic knockout. Then we dragged our captives down into the shadow of the hollow; and Nayland Smith and I clothed ourselves in those hot, stuffy, camel-hair garments.

"Remember the sign," he rapped—"*Si Fan!* . . . then the formal Moslem salute."

"Good enough! But these fellows probably talked Chinese . . ."

"So do I!" he rapped. "Leave that to me." He turned to Weymouth. "Your job is to raise a party inside half an hour. Off you go! Good luck, Petrie. I count on you, Weymouth."

But when a thousand and one other things are effaced —including that difficult parting—I shall always retain my memories of the moment, when Nayland Smith and I, wearing the cowled robes of the monks, approached that iron-studded door.

My companion was a host in himself; his splendid audacity stimulated. I thought, as he raised his fist and beat seven times upon the sun-bleached wood, that even if this adventure should conclude the short tale of my life, yet it would not have been ill-spent since I had met and been judged worthy to work with Sir Denis Nayland Smith.

PART THREE

7 *KÂLI*

ALMOST immediately the door opened.

Conscious of the fact that our hoods were practically our only disguise, that neither of us possessed a single Mongol characteristic, I lowered my head apprehensively, glancing up into a pair of piercing eyes which alternately regarded my companion and myself.

The keeper of the door was a tall, emaciated Chinaman!

"*Si Fan*," said Nayland Smith, and performed the salutation.

"*Si Fan*," the doorkeeper replied and indicated that he should enter.

"*Si Fan*," I repeated; and in turn found myself admitted.

The Chinaman closed and bolted the door. I discovered myself to be standing in a little arbour within the gateway. Shadow of the wall lay like a pall of velvet about us, but beyond I saw a garden and moon-lighted pavilions, and beyond that again a courtyard set with orange trees. The house embraced this courtyard, and from mûshrabîyeh windows dim lights shone out. But there was no movement anywhere. No servants were visible, other than the tall, emaciated Chinaman who had admitted us. I clutched my monkish robe, recovering some assurance from the presence of the repeater which I carried in my belt.

Extending a skeleton hand, the keeper of the gate indicated that we were to cross the garden and enter the house.

I had taken my share of ordinary chances, having lived anything but a sheltered life. Yet it occurred to me, as I stood there beside Nayland Smith, looking in the direction of the tree-shaded courtyard, that this was the wildest venture upon which I had ever been launched.

Our wits alone could save us!

In the first place it seemed to me that survival hung upon one slender point: Were the Mongolian monks known personally to anyone in the house? If so, we were lost! The several groups assembled in the café at el-Khârga obviously had been strangers to one another ... out there might be—must be—some central figure to whom they were all known.

We had searched the Tibetans for credentials but had found none. And now, suddenly, shockingly, I remembered something!

"Sir Denis!" We had begun to pace slowly across the garden. "We're trapped!"

"Why?" he jerked.

"The elder of those monks wore a queer silver ring on his index finger, set with a big emerald. I noticed it as I helped to tie him up."

Nayland Smith shot his hand out from a loose sleeve of the camel-hair garment. I saw the emerald glittering on his index finger!

"His evidence of identity?" he suggested. "It *was!*"

We crossed the courtyard in the direction of an open doorway. I saw a lobby lighted by one perforated brass lamp swung on chains. There were doors right and left —both of them closed.

On a divan a very old Chinaman was seated. He wore a little cap surmounted by a coral ball. His wizened face was rendered owlish in appearance by the presence of tortoiseshell-rimmed glasses. A fur-trimmed robe enveloped his frail body, his ethereal hands relaxed upon crossed knees. I saw that on an index finger he wore just such a ring as that which Nayland Smith had taken from the Tibetan monk! A silver snuff-bowl rested upon the divan beside him; and as we entered:

"*Si Fan,*" he said in a high, thin voice.

Nayland Smith and I went through the prescribed formula. Whereupon, the Chinaman spoke rapidly to my companion in what I presumed to be Chinese, and extended his right hand.

Nayland Smith stooped, raised the emaciated hand, and with the ring upon its index finger touched his brow, his lips, his breast.

Again, the high, sibilant voice spoke; and Sir Denis extended his own hand. The ritual was repeated—this time, by our singular host. To my intense relief, I realized that I had been taken for granted. Evidently I was a mere travelling companion of my more distinguished compatriot.

Raising a little hammer, the aged Chinaman struck a gong which stood beside him. He struck it *twice.* The door right of the divan opened.

He inclined his head, we both acknowledged the salute and, Smith leading, walked in at the open doorway. As we crossed the threshold he fell back a step, and:

"The Mandarin Ki Ming!" came a whisper close to my ear. "Pray heaven he hasn't recognized me!"

I found myself in a large saloon, scantily furnished as was the lobby. At the further end, approached by three carpeted steps were very handsome double doors, beautifully carved and embellished with semiprecious stones in the patient Arab manner. The place was lighted by a sort of chandelier hung from the centre of the ceiling: it consisted of seven lamps. There were divans around the walls and two deep recesses backed by fine, carven windows.

Seven black cushions placed upon silk-covered mattresses were set in a crescent upon the polished floor, the points of the crescent toward the double doors. Beside each mattress stood a little coffee table.

Four of the mattresses were occupied and in the following order:

That on the left point of the crescent by the tall distinguished-looking man whom Nayland Smith had surmised to be a Turk; the second by two of the Burmans I had seen in the café. Then, centre of the crescent, were three vacant places. The next mattress was occupied by the Afghans, and that on the right horn of the crescent by the appalling *thugs*.

Four of the Seven were present. We, fifth to arrive, had been announced by only *two* strokes of the gong.

Which of those three vacant places were we intended to occupy?

This difficulty was solved by the hitherto invisible custodian of the door—who now proved to be a gigantic Negro. Bowing reverently, he led us to the mattress adjoining that of the Afghans. As we crossed, the four groups assembled stood up unanimously, the leaders each raising a right hand upon which I saw the flash of emeralds.

"*Si Fan!*" they cried together.

"*Si Fan*," Nayland Smith replied.

We took our seats.

§2

ONE OF the most dreadful-looking old men I had ever seen in my life entered to the sound of three gongs. As cries of "*Si Fan*" died away, he took his place on the mattress one removed from ours. He was a Syrian, I thought, and of incalculable age. His fiercely hooked nose had a blade-like edge and from under tufted white brows hawk eyes surveyed the assembly with an imperious but murderous regard.

Beyond doubt this was the Sheikh Ismail, lineal successor of the devilish Sheikh al-Jébal, and lord of the *Hashishîn!*

Upon ourselves, particularly, that ferocious gaze seemed to linger. The atmosphere was positively electrical. It contained, I believe, enough evil force to have destroyed a battalion. I simply dared not contemplate what our fate would be in the event of discovery. Our lives were in the hands of Weymouth and Petrie!

One place remained—that in the centre of the crescent. A gong sounded—*once*.

I realized that having admitted the mandarin, the

Negro doorkeeper had retired and closed the door. A hush of expectancy came. Then, from somewhere beyond the end of the saloon a silver bell sounded . . . seven times, and the beautiful doors swung open.

A woman appeared at the top of the steps, facing us but backed by shadow. . . .

Her hair was entirely concealed beneath a jewelled headdress. She wore jewels on her slim, bare arms. A heavy girdle which glittered with precious stones supported a grotesquely elaborate robe, sewn thickly with emeralds. From proudly raised chin to slight, curving hips she resembled an ivory statue of some Indian goddess. Indeed, as I watched, I knew she was Kâli, wife of Siva and patronne of *Thugs* and *Dacoits,* from whom they derived their divine right to slay!

All heads were lowered and a word sounding like a shuddering sigh, but to me unintelligible, passed around the assembly.

I was fascinated—hypnotized—carried out of myself—as from under the sheltering cowl I looked and looked . . . into those brilliant jade-green eyes of Kâli . . . *Madame Ingomar!*

We had posed ourselves in imitation of the other groups: Nayland Smith reclining beside the black cushion so that his elbow could rest upon it, and I crouching behind him. Any exchange of words at that moment was impossible.

In such a silence that I believe one could have heard the flight of a moth, Fah Lo Suee began to speak. She spoke first in Chinese, then in Turkish, of which I knew a few words. Her audience was spell-bound. Her silver bell voice had a hypnotic quality utterly outside the range of my experience. She employed scarcely any gesture. Her breathing could not visually be detected. That slender body retained its ivory illusion. The spell lay in her voice . . . and in her eyes.

She uttered a phrase in Arabic.

Two strokes of a gong sounded from behind me.

The Mandarin Ki Ming stood up. Fah Lo Suee ceased speaking—and I heard the high, sibilant tones of the Chinaman.

I saw Sheikh Ismail leap to his feet like the old panther he was. I saw his blood-lustful gaze fixed upon mine.

We were discovered! *Two gong strokes!*

The real Tibetans had escaped—were here!

A sickly sweet exotic perfume came to my nostrils. I experienced a sudden sense of pressure. . . .

§ 3

THE ILLUSION persisted. It seemed to have recurred at intervals for many nights and days, many weeks—for an immeasurable period. . . .

Always, that vague exotic perfume heralded the phase. This, invariably, seemed to arouse me from some state of unconsciousness in which I thought I must have been suspended for long ages. Once, I became victim of a dreadful idea that I had solved the mystery of perpetual life but was condemned to live it in a tomb. . . .

Then, next, I saw her—the green goddess with eyes of jade. I knew that her smooth body was but a miraculous gesture of some Eastern craftsman immortalized in ivory; that her cobra hair gleamed so because of inlay and inlay of subtly chosen rare woods: her emerald robe I knew for an effect of cunning light, her movements for a mirage.

But when she knelt beside me, the jade-green eyes held life—cold ivory was warm satin. And slender insidious hands, scented lotus blossoms, touched me caressingly. . . .

At last came true awakening—and memories.

Where was I? Obviously, I must be in the house of the Sheikh Ismail where the Council of Seven had met. I lay on a divan propped up with many cushions, in a room small enough to have been called a cabinet.

If it were day or night I had no means of judging. Heavy plush curtains of green and gold completely obscured what I assumed to be the window. And I felt as weak as a kitten. In fact, when I tried to sit up in order to study my strange surroundings, I failed to do so.

What had happened to me?

I saw that the floor was covered with a thick green

carpet, and directly facing the divan on which I lay was a magnificent ormolu piece occupying the whole of one wall. A square lamp or lantern hung from the centre of the ceiling and flooded the room with amber light.

An ebony carved chair, evidently of Chinese workmanship, stood near me beside a glass-topped table upon which were phials, instruments, and other surgical items!

Weakly, I looked down at my body. I wore unfamiliar silk pajamas and on my feet were soft Chinese slippers!

What in heaven's name had happened to me?

Now, memory began to function. . . .

Nayland Smith!

I remembered! I remembered! We had been betrayed —or had betrayed ourselves at that incredible meeting of the Council outside el-Khârga! I recalled the high, soft voice of the dreadful mandarin who had denounced us; the staring eyes of the terrible Sheikh. . . . I could recall no more.

Where was Nayland Smith? And where were Petrie and Weymouth?

Some time had clearly elapsed, a fact to which my inexplicable change of attire bore witness. But why had no rescue been attempted? Good God!—a truly horrible doubt came—Weymouth and Petrie had fallen into a trap!

They had never reached el-Khârga!

A dreadful certainty followed. They were dead! I alone had been spared for some unknown reason; and apparently I had been, and still remained, very ill.

Inch by inch—in some way I seemed to have lost the power of coördinating my muscles—I turned, seeking a view of that side of the room which lay behind me. All I saw was a flat green door set in the dull gold of the wall. There was a second such door, which I had already noted, immediately before me.

As I reverted, laboriously, to my previous position the latter door opened. It was a sliding door.

A Chinaman came in! He wore a long white coat of the kind used by hospital attendants. He closed the door behind him.

One swift look I ventured—noting that he was a comparatively young man with a high intellectual forehead, that he wore black-rimmed spectacles and carried a notebook. Then I closed my eyes and lay still.

He took the chair beside me, raised my wrist, and felt the pulse. As he dropped my hand I ventured on a quick glance. He was recording the pulse in his notebook.

Next, unbuttoning the jacket of my silk pajamas, he inserted a clinical thermometer under my left armpit and, leaving it there, dipped the point of a syringe into a glass of water and carefully wiped it on a piece of lint. This, also, I witnessed, without being detected.

Engrossed in his tasks, he was not watching me. I saw him load a shot of some nameless drug into the syringe and place his loaded syringe on the table.

I reclosed my eyes.

The Chinese surgeon removed the thermometer and recorded my temperature.

There was a long, silent interval. I kept my eyes closed. Something told me that he was intrigued, that he was studying me.

Presently, I felt his head close to my bare chest. He pressed his ear against my heart. I lay still, until:

"Ah, Mr. Greville," he said, with scarcely a trace of accent, "you are feeling better, eh?"

I opened my eyes.

The Chinaman was still watching me. His face was quite expressionless as his tones had been.

"Yes," I said . . . and my voice refused to function higher than a whisper!

"Good." He nodded. "I was becoming anxious about you. It is all right now. The artificial nourishment, I think, we may dispense with. Yes, I think so. Do you feel that some very savoury soup and perhaps a small glass of red wine would be acceptable?"

"Definitely!"

My whispering voice positively appalled me!

"I will see to it, Mr. Greville."

"Tell me," I breathed, "where is Nayland Smith?"

The Chinese surgeon looked puzzled.

"Nayland Smith?" he echoed. "I know no one of that name."

"He's here . . . in el-Khârga!"

"El-Khârga?" He stopped and patted me on the shoulder. "I understand. Do not think about this. I will see that you are looked after."

§4

A LITTLE, wrinkled Asiatic, who either was deaf and dumb or who had had orders to remain silent, brought me a bowl of steaming soup and a glass of some kind of light Burgundy. It was a vegetable soup, but excellent, as was the wine.

And presently I found myself alone again.

I listened intently, trying to detect some sound which should enable me to place the location of this extraordinary green and gold room in which I found myself. Any attempt to escape was out of the question. I was too weak to stir from the divan.

Apart from a vague humming in my aching head, no sound whatever could I hear.

Was I in the house of the Sheikh Ismail? Or had I been smuggled away to some other place in the oasis? An irresistible drowsiness began to creep over me. Once, I aroused with a start which set my heart beating madly.

I thought I had heard a steamer's siren!

Of course (I mused) I had been dreaming again. A sudden, acute anger and resentment stirred me. I was thinking of my companions. I groaned because of my great weakness. . . . I dozed.

Good heavens! What was that?

My heart beating wildly, I tried to sit up. Surely a motor horn! I lay there sweating from the shock of the effort.

I closed my weary eyes. . . .

Divining, rather than knowing, that the door behind me had opened, I kept my lids lowered—but watched.

A faint perfume—which I later determined was rather an aura than a physical fact—reached me. I knew it. This was the herald of another of those troubled visions—visions of the goddess Kâli incarnated.

She stood beside me.

The mythical robes—perhaps never more than figments

of delirium—were not there. She wore a golden Chinese dress not unlike a pajama suit and little gold slippers. The suit was silk of so fine a texture that as she stood between me and the light I could detect the lines of her ivory body as though she floated in a mist of sunrise.

A soft hand touched my forehead.

I raised weary lids and looked up into jade-green eyes. She smiled and dropped into the chair.

So it was Madame Ingomar that I had to thank for my escape!

"Yes," she answered softly in her strange bell-like voice. "I saved your life at great peril to my own."

But I had not spoken!

Her hand caressed my brow.

"I can tell what you are thinking," she said. "I have been listening to your thoughts for so long. When you are strong again, it will not be so—but now it is."

Her voice and her touch were soothing—magnetic. I found my brain utterly incapable of resentment. This woman, kin of the super-devil, Fu Manchu, my enemy, enemy of all I counted worth while—petted me as a mother pets her child!

And a coldness grew in my heart—yet I remained powerless to resist the spell—because I realized that if she willed me not to hate, but to love her, I should obey . . . I could not refuse!

I dragged my gaze away from hers. Irresistible urges were reaching me from those wonderful eyes, which had the brightness of polished gems.

She stooped and slipped her arm under my head.

"You have been very ill," she whispered. Her lips were almost touching me. "But I have nursed you because I am sorry. You are so young and life is good. I want you to live and love and be happy. . . ."

I struggled like a bird hypnotized by a snake. I told myself that her silver voice rang false as the note of a cracked bell; that her eyes were hideous in their unfathomable evil; that her red lips would give poisoned kisses; that her slenderness was not that of a willow but of a poised serpent. And then, as a worshipper calls on

his gods, I called on Rima, conjuring up a vision of the
sweet, grave eyes.

"The little Irish girl is charming," said that bell voice.
"No one shall harm her. If it will make you happy, you
shall have her. . . . And you must not be angry, or get
excited. You may talk to me for a few minutes and then
you must sleep. . . ."

§ 5

MY NEXT awakening was a troubled one. The strange
room looked the same. But *she* had gone. How long? . . .

I had lost all track of time.

What had I imagined and what was real?

Had I asked her, or only dreamed that I had asked
her, of the fate of my friends? I thought I had done so
and that she had told me they were alive, but had refused
to tell me more.

Alive—and, I could only suppose, prisoners!

She had assured me, unemotionally, one arm pillowing
my head and those magnetic fingers soothing my hot
brow, that it was blind folly to oppose her. She wielded
a power greater than that of any potentate living. Her
strange soul was wrapped up in world politics. Russia,
that great land "stolen by fools," was ripe for her purpose. . . .

The present rulers? Pooh! Her specialists (calmly she
spoke of them and I supposed her to mean professional
assassins) would clear away such petty obstacles. Russia
awaited a ruler. The ruler had arisen. And, backed by a
New Russia, which then would be part and parcel of
Asia—"*my* Asia" . . .

China, after many generations, was to be united again.
Japan, in the Far East, Turkey, in the Near East, must
be forced into submission. Already the train was laid.
Kemal stood in her way. Swâzi Pasha, his secret adviser,
must be removed. . . .

"But I am so lonely, Shan. Your name is sweet to me,
because it is like my own Chinese. Sometimes I know I
am only a woman, and that all I see before me ends in
nothing if it brings me only power and no love."

Now I was alone.

This was a superwoman into whose hands I had fallen!
And what blindness had been upon me during our
earlier if brief association to close my eyes to the fact
that she had conceived a sudden, characteristically Oriental infatuation?

Perhaps a natural modesty. I had never been a woman's
man and counted myself negligible when female favours
were being distributed. Or, possibly, my preoccupation
with Rima. Certainly, from the first moment I had met
her, I had not so much as noticed any other woman's
existence or bothered myself to wonder if any other
woman had noticed mine.

Yet, as I recalled again and again, Madame Ingomar
had chosen me to show her over the excavation and had
sought me out many times. Yes, I had been blind. . . .

Now, too late, I saw.

Beyond any dispute, she sprang from generations of
autocrats; power was in her blood. She had selected me,
for no reason that I could imagine; and I had read in
those strange green eyes, as clearly as though she had
spoken, that if I rejected her I must die!

I knew, also, intuitively, that she had experienced love.
Judged by Western standards, she was young. But
judged by any standards she was old in knowledge. However I chose, my triumph would be a short one.

So musing, and as weak as a half-drowned cat, I lay
staring around my gold and green prison.

The door behind me opened and the Chinese doctor
came in.

"Good-morning, Mr. Greville."

I glanced at the heavy curtains. No trace of light
showed through them.

"Good-morning," I said.

My voice was stronger. The Chinaman went through
the ritual of taking pulse and temperature; then:

"A great improvement," he announced. "You have an
admirable constitution."

"But what has been the matter with me?"

He moved his hands in a slight, deprecatory gesture.

"Nothing, in itself, serious: a small injection. But it

was necessary to renew it. . . . However, I am going to get you on your feet, Mr. Greville."

He clapped his hands sharply, and the silent man entered.

Together, and skilfully, they raised me from the divan and carried me into a beautifully equipped bathroom which adjoined the green and gold apartment.

"You must not object to our assistance in your toilet," said the doctor. "Because, although unknown to you, we have so assisted before!"

I submitted to the ordeal of being groomed. I had never been seriously ill, and the business was new to me and utterly detestable. Then I was carried back to bed.

"A lightly boiled egg, and toast," the Chinaman declared, "will not be too severe. Tea—one cup—very weak. . . ."

Presently this was brought and set upon the table beside me. Propped by cushions, I now found it possible to sit up.

With some trace of returning appetite I disposed of this light breakfast. The tray was removed by the dumb man and I lay waiting. Watching the doors alternately, I waited . . . for *her*. And I waited in a steadily mounting horror. In some way which I had never hitherto experienced, this woman, for all her exotic beauty, terrified me.

The door opened . . . the dumb man came in with a number of books, a box of cigarettes, and other small comforts.

There was no clock in the room and my wrist watch had been removed. . . .

I saw no one but this silent Asiatic all day, of the progress of which I could judge only by the appearance of regular meals.

Several times, but more faintly than on the first occasion, I could have sworn I heard river noises, and once what strangely resembled a motor horn.

The Chinese surgeon attended me after I had dealt with a dinner excellently prepared, and "groomed" me for the night. When he had gone, I lay smoking a final cigarette and wondering if . . .

"Turn out the light when you are tired," had been his final injunction.

§6

LYING there in silence and darkness, I almost touched rock bottom. Despair drew desperately near. I was utterly at the mercy of this woman. Whatever had happened to me had left me weaker than a child. And that damnable mystery, the true nature of my illness, was not the least of my troubles.

I suffered no physical pain, except for a throbbing head; I could recall no blow . . . *what* had been done to me?

Sleep was out of the question; but I had tried to find relief from the inexorable amber light. Why, I wondered wearily, had I imagined riverside and street sounds and now imagined them no longer?

And, whilst I turned this problem over in my mind, came a sound which was *not* imaginary.

It was muffled. But I had learned that all sounds reached the green and gold room in that way. Nevertheless, dim though it was, I knew it . . . an eerie minor cry—the cry I had heard in Petrie's courtyard in Cairo. . . .

The call of a Dacoit!

Good God! Had this she-fiend been mocking me! Was I to be strangled as I lay there helpless?

My hand reached out for the switch. I was trembling wildly. Weakness had destroyed my nerve. I grasped it—a pendant—pressed the button. . . .

No light came!

At which I nearly lost myself. I suppose, for the first time in my life, I was delirious, or hysterical.

"Smith!" I cried. "Weymouth! Help! . . ."

My voice was a husky whisper. Weakness and terror had imposed on me that crowning torture of nightmare —inability to summon aid in an emergency.

But this was the peak of my sudden, childish frenzy. The fit passed. Nothing further happened. And I grew cool enough to realize that perhaps my enforced silence had been a blessing in disguise. Smith! Weymouth! . . .

Heaven only knew where my poor friends were at that hour.

The door behind my couch opened.

I lay still—resigned, now, to the inevitable. I did not even attempt to look around, but stayed with half-closed eyes prepared for death.

A dim light appeared.

Watching, I lost faith in myself. I was altogether too exhausted, in my low state, to experience further fear; but I determined that my brain was not so completely to be relied upon as I had supposed. Actually, I was not awake; I hovered between two states in a borderland of hideous fancy.

An outré figure carrying a lantern came into the room. The light of the lantern cast a huge, misshapen image of its bearer on the golden wall.

This was a hunchbacked dwarf—epicene, revolting. His head was of more than normal size; his gray-black bloated features were a parody of humanity; his eyes bulged, demoniac, from a vast skull. He wore indoor Arab dress, a huge tarboosh crowning his repulsive ugliness.

Never so much as glancing in my direction, he crossed to the door on the other side of the room and went out.

Both doors remained open. Sounds reached me.

First among these I detected voices—subdued but keyed to excitement.

They were voices of delirium, I decided. They spoke a language which conveyed nothing to me.

A man wearing an ill-fitting serge suit and a dark blue turban raced through the room in the wake of the dwarf. He carried an electric torch. Its reflection, diffused from the golden walls, exhibited a yellow, tigerish face, lips curled back and fanglike teeth bared in a sadistic grin. . . .

The Dacoit who had followed me to Cairo!

It was a procession of images created by a disordered brain. Yet I was unconscious of any other symptoms of fever.

Two kinds of sounds came to me now: the excited voices, growing louder, and a more distant, continuous disturbance difficult to identify. Then came a third.

A pausing shriek quivered through the house . . . and died into wordless gurgling.

The Dacoit reappeared. He carried a short, curved knife, its blade red to the hilt. . . . His squinting, bloodshot eyes fixed themselves upon me. He drew nearer and nearer to the divan upon which I lay helpless.

Out of the babel of voices, one voice detached itself; a harsh, metallic voice. It cried three words.

The Dacoit passed me—and returned by the way he had originally entered.

A sustained, harsh note . . . a flat, surely unmistakable note—that of a *police whistle!*

I smiled in the darkness.

Clearly, high fever had claimed me. But this ghastly delirium must soon end in unconsciousness. I touched my forehead. It was wet, but cold.

The indistinguishable voices grew faint—and died away.

But that queer, remote booming continued.

And now I determined that it came not from the door behind me—that by which the Dacoit had gone out—but from that which faced the foot of the divan . . . the door through which the hunchback had fled.

A dim crash sent ghostly echo messengers through the building.

Shouts followed. But now I could pick out certain words. . . .

"Easy at the landing, sir! Wait for me . . ."

A sound of clattering footsteps, apparently on a staircase. . . .

"You take that door! I'll take this!"

Surely I knew that great, deep voice.

More ghostly crashing.

"Nothing here!"

"Next floor!"

A background of excited conversation; then:

"Nayland Smith!" came the great voice—"are you there, sir? Shan Greville! Are you there?"

I *did* know that voice!

"Silence!" it commanded. "Listen!"

In the interval of stillness which followed, I tried to

reply. My heart was beating like a racing engine. My brain had become a circus. And the answering cry died in my throat.

"Carry on!"

Clattering of footsteps was renewed. They were somewhere outside the green-gold room, when:

"God's mercy!"

They had found the hunchback. Sudden silence fell. Subdued voices broke it, until, above them:

"There's another room!" came a cry.

Holding an electric lamp, the speaker burst through the doorway. . . .

Delirium was ended: this was reality!

"Greville!"

"*Weymouth!*" I said faintly and stretched out a shaking hand.

8 SWAZI PASHA ARRIVES

PERHAPS the presence of blue-uniformed and helmeted constables in a measure prepared me. But, looking back, I realize that this anomalous intrusion upon the oasis did not register a hundred per cent of its true force at the time.

I was weak in a degree which I simply couldn't believe or accept. The idea of mirage remained. When they carried me through a queer room adjoining that in which I had suffered—a room where something lay covered by a piece of ornate tapestry torn from the wall—I was still no more than half alive to facts.

That the house of the Sheikh Ismail had been raided in the nick of time was clear enough. What had become of Petrie I failed to imagine, nor could I account for the presence of London policemen. Also, I was dreadfully concerned about Nayland Smith.

Weymouth's appearance—he wore dinner kit—also intrigued me. But I remembered that at least two days had elapsed; and in some way, I supposed wearily, this hiatus must explain these seeming discrepancies.

Then we reached the outside of the house. A big gray car stood before the door. There was a crowd. I saw several constables.

I saw the street. . . .

I saw a long, neglected wall. From a doorway in this wall I had been carried out to the car. Adjoining was a row of drab, two-storied houses. Similar houses faced them from across the narrow way. Some of the doors were open, and in the dim light shining out groups were gathered.

They were Chinese—some of them. Others were nondescript. The crowd about the car, kept in check by two constables, was made up of typical East End London elements!

I was placed comfortably on the cushions. A man whom I suddenly recognized as Fletcher seated himself in front with the chauffeur. Weymouth got in beside me. The car moved off.

"You're all at sea!" he said, and rested his hand reassuringly on my arm. "Don't think too much about it yet. I'm going to take you to Dr. Petrie's hotel. He'll get you on your feet again."

"But . . . where am I?"

"You're in Limehouse at the moment."

"What!"

"Keep cool! You didn't know? Well, it is so."

"But, *two days* back, I was in Egypt!"

As the car swung into a wide, populous thoroughfare— West India Dock Road, I learned later—Weymouth turned to me. His expression, blank at first, gradually changed, and then:

"Good heavens, Greville," he said, "I'm just beginning to understand!"

"I wish *I* could!"

"Brace yourself up—because it's going to be a shock; although the facts must have prepared you for it. You said, which you can see now is impossible, that you were in Egypt two days back. . . . Can you stand the truth? You left Egypt *a month ago!"*

§ 2

A WEEK elapsed. Petrie's treatment worked wonders. And a day came when, looking down from a hotel sitting room on the busy life of Piccadilly, I realized that the raw edges of the thing had worn off.

I had lost a month out of my life. I had been translated in the manner of the old Arabian tales from the Oasis of Khârga to some place in Limehouse. The smooth channel of my ways had been diverted; and the shock of recognizing this had staggered me. But now, as I say, I was reconciled. Also, better equipped to cope with it: indeed, nearly fit again.

"My extraordinary experience with Sir Lionel," said Petrie, who stood just behind me, "was of enormous assistance in your own case, Greville."

"You mean the success of the new treatment suggested by Sir Brian Hawkins?"

"Yes . . . at least, so I believed."

I turned away from the window and stared at Petrie curiously. His expression puzzled me.

"I don't understand, Doctor. You sent a telegram from Luxor to Sir Brian in London, giving him full details about the chief. He cabled back saying that he had communicated these particulars to a Dr. Amber—a former assistant—who was fortunately then in Cairo and who would ring you up."

"Quite so, Greville. And this Dr. Amber did ring up, discussed the case with me, said he agreed with Sir Brian's suggestion and despatched, express, a small box. It contained a third of a fluid drachm of some preparation, labelled 'One minim per day subcutaneously until normal.' After four injections, Sir Lionel fully recovered —except that he had no recollection of what had taken place from the time of the attack to that when he opened his eyes in his room at the Luxor hotel."

"That's plain sailing enough, Petrie, and a big success for Sir Brian Hawkins. You came to the conclusion that

I was suffering from the effects of overdoses of the same drug—"

"And so I tried the same cure—with equally marvellous results."

He paused, staring me hard in the face; then:

"When we got down to Cairo," he went on—"as you know, I postponed sailing—Dr. Amber had left his hotel. And when we reached London, Sir Brian Hawkins was abroad. He came home this morning."

"Well?" I said, for he had paused again, staring at me in that peculiar manner.

"Sir Brian Hawkins never received my telegram."

"What!"

"He was unacquainted with anyone called Dr. Amber —and the preparation, a specimen of which I had taken with me, was totally unknown to him!"

"Good God!"

"Don't let it worry you, Greville. We've been the victims of a cunning plot. But the unknown plotter has saved two valuable lives—and defeated Fah Lo Suee! Excuse me if I run away now. Please stay here and make yourself at home. My wife wants to do some shopping, and I never allow her out alone, even in London. You know why," he added significantly.

I nodded, as:

"Rima and Sir Lionel are due to-morrow," he said, "and I know how you're counting the hours."

§ 3

So WHILST it was true that to Petrie and to Weymouth I owed the fact that I now stood staring down again on the busy life of Piccadilly, I owed even more to . . . someone else! I was all but fit. I had taken a stroll in the Park, and with decent precautions for a week or two was competent to reënter the battle of life. But—who was Dr. Amber?

Almost a deeper mystery than that of the hiatus, to me represented by a blank in my existence; and this, heaven knows, was strange enough!

The house of the Sheikh Ismail had been raided by a party under the mudîr of Khârga. This official, it seems, was already suspicious of the strange visitors to the town.

They found not a soul on the premises!

El-Khârga was combed carefully. No trace. The mudîr got in touch with Esna, and all roads were watched. Nothing resulted. The dreadful Seven had dispersed—into thin air! Nayland Smith was missing, I was missing; and Said had disappeared with the car. . . .

Weymouth set the official wires humming. Too late, it had occurred to him that Fah Lo Suee might have retired not upon Esna but upon Asyût. Later, this theory was proved to be the correct one.

A dead man, a piece of baggage, I had been carried across the desert to Asyût, entrained for Port Said, and shipped to England, as cargo is shipped! Three days too late to hold her in the Egyptian port, Weymouth, inspecting the books of the Suez Canal Company, discovered that a Clyde-built steamer chartered by a Chinese firm for some private enterprise had passed through the Canal and cleared Port Said at a date which corresponded with his suspicions. Radio was set humming all over the Mediterranean; and the suspected craft was finally boarded off Cherbourg by the French police.

Her papers were in order; but consignments of goods and a number of her people had already been despatched overland.

This was the state of affairs when the party reached England. Weymouth, of course, had secured leave of absence in the circumstances; and acting upon the policy adopted by poor Nayland Smith in earlier days, had succeeded with the backing of Scotland Yard in keeping all publicity out of the press.

It was the efficiency of Detective-Inspector Yale and of K Division which led to my rescue. For some time they had been watching certain premises in the Limehouse area. Apart from consignments of suspicious goods and of the presence, particularly at night, of Asiatics of a character not usual in that district, a smartly dressed woman had visited the place.

Now, furnished by Weymouth with particulars of those goods sent overland from Cherbourg, Yale secretly inspected some of the crates and packing cases stored in the yard of the suspected premises. As a result of what he found, I was rescued from the green and gold room, and restored to health by Dr. Petrie. But a shadow lay upon all of us—one indeed, which had retarded my convalescence.

§ 4

"Our last battle against Fu Manchu," said Weymouth sadly, "has opened with a big score for the enemy. We've lost our field-marshal."

Detective-Inspector Yale nodded gloomily. I had met him several times before, and I knew that with Fletcher he had been put in charge of this case, which, in his eyes, had neither beginning nor end.

"It's a blank mystery to me," he confessed. "Excepting one badly murdered dwarf, there wasn't a thing of any use to us in the Limehouse raid."

"You're rather overlooking *me!*"

Detective-Inspector Yale smiled; Weymouth laughed aloud.

"Sorry, sir," said Yale. "But the fact remains—we drew blank. The house was undoubtedly used by these *Si Fan* people. But where *are* they? I knew when Sir Denis took personal control there was something serious in the wind. He was overdue leave, it's true, but he was a demon for work; and I saw when he started for Egypt with Fletcher he'd gone for business, not pleasure. Besides, there was a big dossier accumulating."

He smiled again, turning slightly in my direction.

"The death of Professor Zeitland was a bad show for the Yard," he admitted. "It was long after the event that we realized his death wasn't due to natural causes. This in strict confidence, Mr. Greville. There's been no publicity about the absence of Sir Denis, because we've kept on hoping from day to day, and his instructions on that point were explicit. But personally . . ."

He turned aside and stared out of the window.

"I'm afraid so," Weymouth whispered.

"It's a job," Yale went on, "which I admit is above my weight. Most extraordinary reports are accumulating and the Foreign Office has nearly driven me crazy. I never knew very much about this Dr. Fu Manchu, outside the department records. I was just a plain detective officer in those days. But it looks to me—and this is where I am badly out of my depth, Superintendent—as though this delayed visit of Swâzi Pasha comes into the case!"

"I'm sure it does!" I replied. "The woman you knew as Madame Ingomar regards the present rulers of Turkey as her enemies. Swâzi Pasha is probably the biggest man in Stamboul to-day. She told me with her own lips that he was marked!"

"Amazing!" said Yale. "He is to occupy Suite Number 5 in this hotel, and apart from routine measures, I'm going to satisfy myself about the staff."

I accompanied Weymouth and Yale on their tour of inspection. The suite was on the floor below, and we went down the stairs. Yale had the key and we entered. Everything had been prepared for the comfort of the distinguished visitor and his confidential private secretary.

Suite Number 5 consisted of a reception room entered from a lobby, a dining room, and two bedrooms with bathrooms adjoining. Swâzi Pasha had been detained by illness in Paris, so the press informed us, but would arrive at Victoria that evening.

Detective-Inspector Yale seemed to suspect everything in the place. The principal bedroom he explored as though he anticipated discovering there trap doors, sliding panels, or other mediæval devices. He even turned on the electric heater, an excellent imitation of a coal fire, and considered it carefully; until:

"Once he gets here," said Weymouth. "He's safe enough. It's outside that he's in danger."

Yale turned to him, one eyebrow raised interrogatively, and:

"Queer *you* should say that," he replied. "I've been going carefully through the records—and you ought to know better than I do that if we're really up against this Asiatic group the best hotel in London isn't safe!"

I glanced at Weymouth, and saw his expression change.

"True enough," he admitted. "Dr. Fu Manchu got a

man in the New Louvre once, under our very eyes. Yes, you're right."

With enthusiasm he also began to sound walls and to examine fittings, until:

"I have had painful personal evidence of what these people can do," I said, "but I rather agree with Inspector Yale that the danger to Swâzi Pasha is greater outside than here."

Yale turned and:

"Outside," he assured me stolidly, "short of a fanatic who is prepared to pay the price with his life, Swâzi Pasha is as safe as any man in Europe. But in the absence of Sir Denis, I'm responsible for him and, knowing what I know now, I'm prepared for anything."

§5

WHEN presently I left Weymouth and Yale, I became selfishly absorbed in my own affairs again. The chief had engaged rooms by radio for himself and Rima here at the Park Avenue, and as I wandered back to my own apartment I found myself wondering which rooms they were. Indeed, a perfectly childish impulse prompted me to go down and inquire of the office.

As I entered the corridor in which my own quarters were located as well as those of Dr. Petrie and his wife, I saw a figure hurrying ahead of me. Reaching the door next to my own, he inserted and turned the key in the lock. As he did so, I had a view of his face in profile. . . .

Then he went in, and I heard the door shut.

Entering my own room, I sat down on the bed, lighted a cigarette, and wondered why this chance encounter seemed so important. It was striking discords of memory which I couldn't solve. I smoked one cigarette and lighted a second, thinking hard all the time, before the solution came, then:

"I've got it!" I cried.

This man in the next room was the Turk who had attended the Council of Seven!

I glanced at the telephone. This was a mystery completely beyond my powers—something which Weymouth and Yale should know about at once. I hesitated, realizing that in all probability they were on their way to Victoria. A tremendous unrest seized me. What did it mean? That it meant mischief—and bloody mischief—I felt certain. But what should I do?

I lighted a pipe and stared down into Piccadilly. Inaction was intolerable. What *could* I do? I couldn't give this man in charge of the police. Apart from the possibility of a mistake, what evidence had I against him? Finally I grabbed my hat and went out into the corridor. I had detected no sound of movement in the neighbouring room.

Walking over to the lift, I rang the bell. The cage had just arrived and I was on the point of stepping in, when I thought someone passed swiftly behind me.

I turned. My nerves were badly overtuned. The figure had gone, but:

"Who was that?" I said to the lift-boy.

"Who do you mean, sir," he asked. "I didn't see anyone."

I thought that he was looking at me rather oddly, and: "Ground floor," I said.

Had this thing got me more deeply than I realized? Small wonder if it were so, considering my own experience. But was I beginning to imagine creatures of Dr. Fu Manchu, shadows, menaces, where really there was no physical presence? It was a dreadful thought, one to be repelled at all costs by a man who had passed through the nightmare of that month which I had survived.

For I had been dead and I lived again.

Sometimes the horror of it wakened me in the middle of the night. A drug, unknown to Western science, had been pumped into my veins. The skill of an Asiatic physician had brought me back to life. Petrie's experience —aided by the mysterious "Dr. Amber"—had done the rest. But there might be an aftermath, beyond the control even of this dreadful Chinaman whose shadow again was creeping over Europe.

My present intention was to walk across to Cook's and learn at what time the S.S. *Andaman*, in which Sir Lionel and Rima were travelling, docked, and when the boat-train arrived. I was in that state of anxiety in which one ceases to trust that high authority, the hotel hall porter.

This purpose was frustrated by the sudden appearance, as I came down the steps, of Dr. Petrie and his wife. I was instantly struck by the fact that something had terrified Mrs. Petrie. The doctor was almost supporting her. . . .

"Hello, Greville," he said. "My wife has had rather a shock. Come back with us for a minute."

The fact was obvious enough. Filled with a sudden new concern, I realized, as I took Mrs. Petrie's arm and walked back up the hotel steps, that she was in a condition bordering on collapse. Well enough I knew that this could mean only one thing. As I had suspected, as Weymouth had suspected—the enemy was near us!

In the lobby she sat down and her husband regarded her anxiously. Normally, she had the most wonderful flower-like complexion—I mean naturally, without artificial aid—of any woman I had ever met. Now she was pale, and her wonderful eyes mirrored a sort of mysterious horror.

"Are you sure, Kara? Are you sure?" Petrie asked with deep concern.

"Could I ever be wrong about *him?*"

"When you are safely upstairs, dear," he replied, "I am going back to confirm your suspicion—or disprove it."

"But," I exclaimed, "whatever is wrong?"

"*He* is here."

"What do you mean, Mrs. Petrie? *Who* is here?"

She looked up at me, and for all her pallor I knew how beautiful she was. I thought that if those strange, wonderful eyes had beckoned to me before I had known Rima, I should have followed wherever they led. She was, indeed, very lovely, and very terrified; and:

"It seems like madness," she whispered; "but about this I can *never* be mistaken. If I had not seen, I should have felt. But I *saw*."

"Do you understand, Greville," Petrie interrupted tersely, "my wife saw—I can't doubt her; she has never been wrong on this point—someone looking out from a window above a shop in Burlington Arcade."

"I know it is madness, but I know it is true," she said.

"When?" I demanded.

"A moment ago."

"But do you mean—"

Mrs. Petrie nodded.

Her eyes were tragic. She stood up.

"I am going upstairs," she said. "No, truly, I'm quite all right again. Go back, or it may be too late. But take Mr. Greville with you."

She walked towards the lift, whilst Petrie and I watched her. As she entered and the lift went up:

"It seems simply incredible to me," I declared. "But do you mean that in a room over a shop in Burlington Arcade—"

"A dealer in Oriental jewellery, yes!" Petrie took me up quickly. "I could see nothing—the room above was in darkness—but Karamanèh saw *Dr. Fu Manchu* looking down!"

§6

I wondered if Nayland Smith would have approved of Petrie's method of inquiry. Personally, I thought it admirable, for as we entered the establishment, oddly reminiscent, as many are in the Arcade, of a shop in an Eastern bazaar:

"My wife came along this afternoon," said Petrie, "and noticed a large Chinese figure in the room above. She asked me to call and learn the price."

The salesman, who would not have been out of place in any jewel market of the Orient, except for the fact that he wore a well-cut morning coat, raised his eyebrows in surprise. He was leaning upon a case containing typical Levantine exhibits, and all sorts of beaded necklaces framed him about. I thought that, saving the presence of civilized London around us, he might, considered alone, have been termed a sinister figure.

"The room above, sir," he replied, "is not my property. It is used as a store-room by another firm. See"—he turned —"the stair is there, but the door is locked. I have a case upon it as you may observe for yourself. That door is very rarely opened. And I assure you it contains no Chinese figure."

He made no attempt to sell us anything.

But outside, in the Arcade, we both stared up at the window above the shop. The room to which it belonged appeared to be empty. Petrie shrugged.

"She has never been wrong before," he said significantly. "And the gentleman with whom we have been chatting gives one the shudders."

"I agree, but what can we do!"

"Nothing," he replied.

Turning, we walked back to the Park Avenue Hotel. The journey was a short one, but long enough for me to tell Petrie of my encounter in the corridor. He stopped as we reached the corner of Berkeley Street, and:

"There's some very black business underlying all this, Greville," he said. "We've lost the best man of the lot already. Now it looks as though the arch-devil had taken personal charge. Where's Weymouth?"

"Gone to Victoria, I expect. Yale was with him."

Petrie nodded.

"If you weren't mistaken, Greville, it looks as though the danger to Swâzi Pasha is here, in London. If my wife isn't mistaken—it's a certainty! We can at least learn the name of the man you saw; because in dealing with Dr. Fu Manchu and his Burmans I don't believe in coincidences!"

We consulted the reception clerk and learned without difficulty that the room, of which I naturally remembered the number, was occupied by a Mr. Solkel, of Smyrna.

"Has he stayed here before?" Petrie asked.

No. It was Mr. Solkel's first visit.

"Thank you," said Petrie, and as we walked towards the lift:

"Mr. Solkel, of Smyrna," he mused. "I don't like the sound of him."

"*I* don't like the look of him!"

"Yet it is just possible you were wrong; and so—what can we do?"

We went up to Petrie's sitting room where his wife, apparently recovered, was waiting to receive us.

She smiled, her gaze set on Petrie's face; and I wondered if Rima would greet *me* with a smile like that. He simply shook his head and ran his fingers through her beautiful hair.

"I knew," she whispered; and although she continued bravely to smile, there was horror in her eyes. "He is so clever! But I was right!"

A nameless but chill foreboding possessed my mind. I believe the others shared it. I was thinking of the man who had gone out to meet this menace, and had come to his end, alone against many, in that damnable house in Khârga. But, Petrie now ringing for cocktails, we all tried to show a bold front to our troubles. Yet even as I raised my glass I seemed to detect, like a sort of patrol, the approach of *something;* not as a memory, but as words spoken eerily, to hear a bell-like voice:

"I am so lonely, Shan. . . ."

For days and nights, for weeks, I had lain in her power . . . the witch-woman; daughter of this fiend incarnate, Dr. Fu Manchu. "She is evil, evil . . ." Rima had said. And I knew it for truth. Much as we had all suffered, I felt that worse was to come. I could hear the cheery, familiar roar of London's traffic beneath me; sometimes, dimly, I could catch snatches of conversation in the adjoining apartment, occupied by an enthusiastic American traveller and his wife.

Everything was so safe, so normal. Yet I knew, I could not venture to doubt, that some climax in the incredible business which had blotted out a month of my life and had brought Sir Lionel Barton to the edge of eternity, was creeping upon us.

§7

"THANK goodness that part of the business is over," said Weymouth. "There were no official formalities, as the Pasha is still indisposed. He was all silk mufflers and fur collar. He has only one secretary with him. The other members of his suite are staying at the Platz over the way. He's safe indoors, anyway."

"Safe?" Mrs. Petrie echoed and laughed unhappily. "After what I have told you, Superintendent?"

Weymouth's kindly face looked very grim, and he exchanged a troubled glance with Petrie; then:

"She never used to be wrong, Doctor," he confessed. "Honestly, I don't know what to make of it. I sent a man around directly I got the news. But of course the shop was closed and locked. I don't know what to make of it," he repeated. "The woman was rapidly becoming a nightmare to me, but if the Doctor in person has appeared on the scene . . ."

He spread his hands in a helpless gesture; and we were all silent for some time. Then Weymouth stood up:

"It's very nice of you, Mrs. Petrie," he said, "to ask me to dine with you. I have one or two little jobs to do downstairs, first—and I'm going to have another shot to get a look at Mr. Solkel. It isn't really my case." He smiled in the awkwardly boyish manner which made the man so lovable. "But I've been retained as a sort of specialist, and Yale is good enough to be glad."

"I suppose," said Petrie, as Weymouth made for the door, "there are detectives on duty in the hotel?"

"Five, with Fletcher in charge. That should be enough. But I'm worried about Solkel. His official description doesn't correspond with yours, Greville. For one thing, they tell me he wears glasses, is in delicate health, and keeps to his room constantly. However . . ."

He went out.

Petrie stared hard in my direction.

"There's absolutely no doubt," he said slowly, "that Madame Ingomar's campaign has opened well, for her. Her astonishing indiscretion, I can only ascribe to"—he paused, smiling, and glanced at his wife—"a sudden and characteristically Oriental infatuation."

She flushed, glancing at him, and:

"Nayland Smith once said that about *me!*" she replied.

"I'm glad he did!" Petrie returned. "But if the daughter is anything like the father, I confess even now I don't envy Swâzi Pasha's chances. Just check up on madame's record, and you will see what I mean. Apart from certain mysterious movements last year, in such widely divided places as Pekin, Turkestan, Siberia, and the northern provinces of India, we may take it for a fact that Profes-

sor Zeitland fell a victim to this Chinese she-devil. He
stood in her way. He knew something about Lafleur's
Tomb which *she* wanted to know. Having learned it, it
became necessary that he should be blotted out. This
duly occurred, according to schedule. Barton was the
next in her path. He served her purpose and escaped by
a miracle. She got what she wanted—the contents of the
tomb. If we could even guess the importance of these, we
might begin to understand why she stuck at nothing to
achieve her end.'

He paused to light a fresh cigarette, and then:

"I believe poor old Smith *knew*," he went on. "He was
the one man in the world she had *really* to fear. And he
. . ." the sentence remained unfinished.

"That she regarded Swâzi Pasha as an obstruction," I
said, "she was good enough to tell me herself."

Petrie glanced at his wife, whose expressive eyes registered a deep horror; then:

"I said a while ago," he added, "that I don't give very
much for his chances. Selfishly, I can find it in my heart
to wish that he had chosen another hotel. Karamanèh
has lived in the storm centre too long to want any further
experiences.'

This, then, was the atmosphere which surrounded us
all that evening in a London hotel; this the shadow under
which we lay.

During dinner—which was served in Petrie's sitting
room, for Weymouth had had no opportunity of dressing:

"I suppose," said I, "that Mr. Solkel is receiving suitable
attention?"

Weymouth nodded.

"He hasn't gone out," he replied. "But I hear that a
new wardrobe trunk was delivered and taken up to his
room this afternoon. This suggests that he is leaving
shortly. If he goes out he will be followed. If he rings for
anything, the waiter will be a Scotland Yard man.'

Weymouth had secured a small room right up under
the roof, for London was packed. But I drew a great
sense of security from his presence in the building. At his
wife's request, Petrie had abandoned a programme for

the evening, arranged earlier, and had decided to remain
at home.

When we said good-night to our host and hostess,
Weymouth came along to my room. Pausing in the corridor, he stared at the door of Number 41; but not until
we had entered my adjoining apartment and lighted our
pipes, did he speak; then:

"Swâzi Pasha has cancelled an engagement to dine
with the prime minister to-night, owing to the delay in
Paris," he said. "He's not going out and is receiving no
one. Even the press have been refused. But Yale's job
starts to-morrow. The Pasha has four public appointments."

"You feel fairly confident, then, of his safety to-night?"

"Perfectly," Weymouth replied grimly. "I feel so confident about it that I'm going to patrol the hotel in person! You turn in, Greville. You're not really fit yet.
Good-night."

§ 8

SLEEP was a difficult problem. Apart from a morbid and
uncontrollable apprehension, I was intensely strung up by
reason of the fact that Rima was due in the morning. I
tried reading, but simply couldn't concentrate upon the
printed page.

The jade-green eyes of Fah Lo Suee began to haunt
me, and in the dialogue of the story I was trying to read
I seemed to hear her voice, speaking the lines in that
bell-like, hypnotic voice.

I relived those ages of horror and torment in the green-
gold room: I saw again the malignant dwarf—"A *hashi-
shin*," Weymouth had told me. "They belong to the Old
Man of the Mountain—Sheikh Ismail." I heard the creature's dying shrieks; I saw the Dacoit return, carrying his
bloody knife. . . .

Throwing down the magazine disgustedly, I began to
pace my room. I contemplated another whisky-and-soda,
but realized in time that it would be a poor cure for
insomnia. The after-theatre rush was subsiding. Piccadilly
was settling down into its nightly somnolence. That inner
circle of small, expensive streets containing the exclusive

dance clubs would be full of motor traffic now. for London's night life is highly centralized, the Bohemia of Soho impinging on the white-shirted gayety of Mayfair; two tiny spots on the map; sleepless eyes in a sleeping world.

I wondered if Petrie and his wife were awake—and I wondered what Weymouth was doing. This curiosity about Weymouth grew so intense that I determined to ring and find out. It was at this moment that I first heard the sound.

It was difficult to identify. I stood still, listening—all those doubts and surmises centred now upon my mysterious neighbour, Mr. Solkel. What I heard was this:

A dim, metallic sound, which might have been made by someone slightly shaking a sheet of thin metal. Next, a faint sibilance, which oddly suggested paying out a line. Then came silence. . . .

My brain was functioning at high pressure. Whereas, in the foggy stage that followed my dreadful experience, I should have been incapable of thinking consistently about anything, now a dozen theories sprang to my mind. I decided to stand still—and to listen.

The sound was renewed. It came from beyond the fireplace!

An electric radiator, which I had had no occasion to use, stood there. Stooping, I quietly placed it on the rug; and kneeling down I pressed my ear to the tiles of the recess in which it had rested.

Whispering!

And at this very moment a fact occurred to me . . . a startling fact!

My room was directly above Suite Number 5!

The connection defied me, but of one thing I was sure: these strange noises, which had temporarily ceased, portended some attempt on Swâzi Pasha's apartments below.

I came to a swift decision. Walking silently in my slippers, I crossed to the door, opened it cautiously, and peeped out into the corridor. It was empty and dark save for one dim light at the end. Leaving my door ajar, I started for the staircase. . . .

A sense of urgency possessed me—I must find Wey-

mouth or Fletcher! The fate not only of a Turkish states-
man but perhaps of Europe depended upon promptitude.

Silence everywhere as I hurried along the corridor to
the staircase. I raced down in semi-darkness. I reached
the corridor below, lighted only by one dim lamp just
above the elevator shaft. I looked right. The corridor was
empty. I looked left. There was no one.

Hesitant, I stood debating my course. I might ring for
the lift-man. I might race on down into the lobby and
summon the night porter. The result would have been
better accomplished had I used my own room telephone.
No doubt I had counted too confidently on meeting
Fletcher or Weymouth.

I determined to take the matter into my own hands. I
turned left, and walked swiftly in the direction of the
door of Suite Number 5.

Even at the moment that I reached it I hesitated again.
Of the fact that some deadly peril, urgent, instant,
threatened Swâzi Pasha, I seemed to have occult information. But, as I realized, my facts were scanty. If I roused
him, I might save his life. On the other hand, I might
make myself ridiculous.

There was a bell-push outside the door, and my hand
was raised to press it. Suddenly, silently, the door opened
. . . and I found myself staring into the gaunt, angular
face of *Nayland Smith!*

9 THE MAN FROM EL-KHĀRGA

WITH one significant gesture, Nayland Smith silenced the
words on my lips. He took a quick step forward into the
corridor and I saw that he was barefooted. Then, his lips
very close to my ear:

"Lucky I heard you," he whispered. "One ring would
have ruined everything! Come in. Be silent. . . . Whatever happens, do nothing."

He stepped back, pointing urgently to my slippers. I removed them and tiptoed into the lobby. Nayland Smith reclosed the front door without making a sound and led me into the principal bedroom.

Except for a faint streak of light coming through the curtains, the room was in darkness. He pushed me down into a corner near the foot of the bed and disappeared.

To say that I was astounded would be to labour the obvious. I actually questioned my sanity. That Nayland Smith was alive made me want to shout with joy. But what in heaven's name was he doing in Swâzi Pasha's apartments? Where had he been and why had he failed to notify us of his escape? Finally, what was it that I had nearly ruined by my unexpected appearance and for what was he waiting in the dark?

Where Smith had gone and why we were concealing ourselves, I simply couldn't imagine; but, my eyes growing used to the gloom, I peered carefully about the bedroom without moving from the position in which he had placed me. I could see no one, hear nothing.

Then all my senses became keyed up—alert. I had detected a sound of soft footsteps in the corridor outside! I waited—listening to it drawing nearer and nearer. The walker had reached the door, I thought . . . But he did not pause, but passed on. The sound of footsteps grew faint—and finally died away.

Silence fell again. The window behind those drawn curtains was open at the top, and sometimes faint street noises reached my ears: the hooting of a passing taxi, the deeper note of a private car; and once, rumbling of what I judged to be a string of heavy lorries.

But in the building about me, complete silence prevailed. I found myself looking across an eiderdown bedspread in the direction of the fireplace. Except that it was more ornate, it closely resembled that in my own room. The shock of meeting Smith, the present horrible mystery, keyed up my already wide-awake brain. I began to form a theory. . . .

At which moment, as if to confirm it, came a faint sound. Something was shuffling lightly behind the electric radiator!

This was backed by green tiles, or imitation tiles which I judged to be stamped on metal. The deep recess which they lined resembled a black cavity from where I crouched. I could just detect one spot of light on the metal hood of the radiator.

Following some moments of tense silence, came a second sound. And this ... I recognized.

It was the same subdued, metallic clang which had arrested my attention in the room above!

I thought that the darkness behind the radiator had grown even denser. I scarcely breathed. Fists clenched, I watched, preparing to duck if any light should come, since my discovery was clearly the last thing Nayland Smith desired.

The spot of high light on the hood moved outwards, towards me. I was afraid to trust my sight—until a very soft padding on the carpet provided an explanation of this phenomenon.

Someone had opened the back of the fireplace and now was lifting the radiator out bodily....

Who, or what, had crept out into the room?

Nothing moved again, but I thought a figure stood between me and the recess. Whatever it might be, it remained motionless, so that, after I had concentrated my gaze, it presently took shape in the dusk—but such horrible shape, that, divided only by the width of the bed from it, I shrank involuntarily.

It was a spiritual as well as a physical shrinking, such as I had experienced in that room in Limehouse, when, on the night of horror which had led to my release, a ghastly yellow dwarf had crossed my room, carrying a lantern. Of the fate of that misshapen thing I had seen bloody evidence. This figure now standing silent in the darkness—standing so near to me—was another of the malignant killers; one of those Arabian abominations attached to the Old Man of the Mountain ... he whose blazing eyes, as he sprang up from his mattress when the Mandarin Ki Ming denounced us, formed my last memory of the Council of Seven. ...

A sickly sweet exotic perfume stole to my nostrils. ...

I knew it!

To crouch there inactive with definite terror beginning to claim me was next to impossible; and I wondered why Nayland Smith had imposed so appalling a task. I wondered where he was—I wondered if he had seen what *I* could see—knew what I knew.

The answer came swiftly, almost silently. I heard a dull, nauseating thud, followed by a second, heavier thud on the carpet. Nayland Smith's voice came in a tense whisper:

"Don't stir, Greville."

My heart was beating like a sledge-hammer.

§ 2

I BEGAN to count the seconds. . . . Fully a minute passed in absolutely unbroken silence.

Nayland Smith, I realized now, had been concealed in one of two recesses flanking the projecting fireplace. This same formation occurred in my own room, and might betoken a girder or platform, or possibly a flue. Formerly, the Park Avenue had been fitted with open coal fires.

Another minute passed. Nothing happened. The suspense began to grow intolerable. A third minute commenced—then a sound broke that electric stillness; a soft shuffling sound, like that which had heralded the approach of the Arabian dwarf. It was all the more obvious now since the back of the fireplace had been displaced, and it resembled that of a heavy body moving in a narrow space.

Sounds of movement grew suddenly louder and then ceased altogether.

Silence fell again. This, I believe, was the least endurable moment of all. Every sense told me that someone was peering out into the room. But I hadn't the slightest idea what to expect—nor, if attack were coming, what form it would take!

Soft padding.

Silence.

A whispered phrase came like a hiss out of the darkness:

"*Enta raih fên?*" (Where has he gone?)

The words were Arab—but not spoken by an Arab!

Yet I gathered that the speaker, in what I judged to be a state of excitement, had abandoned his own tongue in favour of that of the murderous dwarf, whose absence clearly puzzled him. But I had little time for thought.

There came a rush, and a crash which shook the room . . . a shot!—a flash of dim light and the tinkle of broken glass! The bullet had shattered the window above my head. . . . Then:

"The switch, Greville!" came Nayland Smith's voice. "Over the bed!"

I sprang up as well as my cramped limbs would permit, jumped onto the bed, and groped for the pendant switch.

A sound of panting and gurgling came from somewhere down on the carpet between the bed and the fireplace; loud banging on the floor. Presently I found the switch, and was dazzled when the room became flooded with light. I jumped across to the other side of the bed. I could hear racing footsteps in the corridor outside, excited voices, movement all about. . . .

At my feet sprawled a man in pajamas, his head thrown back and his eyes staring upward, almost starting from their sockets. Nayland Smith knelt upon him, his right hand clutching the throat of the prostrate man, his left pressing to the floor sinewy brown fingers in which a pistol was gripped.

"Get his gun!" he snapped, without releasing that strangle-hold.

I slipped around the combatants and snatched the pistol from that virile grasp. As I stooped, I had my first proper view of the captive. . . .

He was the man I had seen in the corridor—Mr. Solkel!

A bell was ringing furiously. Someone was banging on the outer door.

"Open!" Smith panted.

Half under the bed lay the hideous dwarf, motionless. Weymouth's voice was raised outside in the corridor now.

"Hello, there!" he bellowed. "Open this door! Be quick, or we shall have to force it!"

"Open!" Smith rapped irritably.

I turned and ran to the door.

One glance of incredulity Weymouth gave; then, followed by Fletcher and two others who wore the Park Avenue livery, he rushed past me.

"Good God!" I heard. "Sir Denis!" Then: "Are you mad, sir? You're strangling *Swâzi Pasha!*"

§3

"Our first captures!" said Nayland Smith.

An overcoated figure in charge of two detectives dressed as footmen disappeared from the suite.

"Your mistake, Weymouth, was natural enough. In appearance he *is* Swâzi Pasha."

"He is," said Dr. Petrie, who had joined us in the apartment—all the hotel had been aroused by the shot. "I met Swâzi in Cairo only a year ago; and if the man under arrest is *not* Swâzi Pasha, then I shall never trust my eyes again."

"Really, Petrie?" said Nayland Smith, and smiled in that way which lent him such a boyish appearance. "Yet" —he pointed to the open fireplace—"the metal back of this recess has been removed very ingeniously. It has been reattached to the opening which it was designed to mask, but to-night as you see it hangs down in the ventilation shaft by reason of the fact that a stout piece of canvas has been glued to the back so as to act as a hinge.

"Can you suggest any reason why Swâzi Pasha should remove the back of his fireplace and why he should climb down a rope ladder from the apartment of a certain Mr. Solkel in the middle of the night?"

It was Weymouth who answered the question, and:

"I admit I can't, Sir Denis," he said.

"No wonder! The details of this amazing plot are only beginning to dawn upon me by degrees. In addition to the ladder which undoubtedly communicates with Room 41 above us, there's this stout length of rope with a noose at the end. Can you imagine what purpose it was intended to serve?"

We all stared into the recess. As Smith had said, and as we all had noticed, such a ladder as he described hung in the shaft, possibly as a means of communication between the two floors. A length of rope had been carried into the room. The noose with which it ended lay upon the carpet at our feet.

"I shall make a suggestion," Smith went on. "Mr. Solkel has been occupying Number 41, I understand, for a week past. He has employed his time well! We shall find that the imitation tiling at the back of his fireplace has been removed in a similar fashion to this . . . because Suite Number 5 was reserved for Swâzi Pasha as long as a month ago. The purpose of the ladder is obvious enough. A moment's consideration will convince us, I believe, of the use to which this noose was intended to be put. The business of the dwarf, a highly trained specialist—now in Vine Street Police Station—was quietly to enter Swâzi Pasha's room and to silence him with a wad of cotton-wool which you recall he clutched in his hand, and which was saturated with some narcotic. The smell is still perceptible. Possibly you, Petrie, can tell us what it is?"

Petrie shook his head doubtfully; but:

"I have preserved it," he said. "It's upstairs. Some preparation of Indian hemp, I think."

"*Cannabis indica* was always a favourite, I seem to recall, with this group," Smith said grimly. "Probably you are right. The pasha being rendered quietly unconscious, it was the duty of the dwarf to slip the noose under his arms and to assist the man waiting in the room above to haul the body up. These dwarfs, of whom the first living specimen now lies in a cell in Vine Street—the only *hashishîn*, I believe, ever captured by European police —have the strength of gorillas, although they are of small stature. The body of the insensible man being carried up to Number 41 by the dwarf on the rope ladder, assisted by the efforts of 'Mr. Solkel' above, the pasha was to be placed in bed. Once there, no doubt it was their amiable intention to dispose of him in some manner calculated to suggest that he had died of heart failure.

"Sokel would have taken his place.

"The distressing death of an obscure guest from Smyrna would have been hushed up as much as possible by the hotel authorities—and Mr. Solkel would have lunched with the prime minister in the morning. I am even prepared to believe that the back of the fireplace in Number 41 would have been carefully replaced; although I fail to see how the same could have been done for this one. The dwarf, no doubt, would have been despatched by the new pasha in a crate as a piece of baggage to some suitable address."

"But how did the dwarf get in?" I exclaimed.

"Almost certainly in the wardrobe trunk which Mr. Solkel received to-day," Weymouth answered.

"You're right," Smith confirmed.

"But," I cried, "how could the impostor, granting his extraordinary resemblance to Swâzi Pasha, have carried on?"

"Quite easily," Smith assured me. "He knew all that Swâzi knew. He was perfectly familiar with the latter's movements and with his peculiarly secluded life. He was intimately acquainted with his domestic affairs."

"But," said Petrie, "who *is* he?"

"Swâzi Pasha's twin brother," was the astounding reply; "his deadly enemy, and a member of the Council of Seven."

"But the real Swâzi Pasha?"

"Is at the Platz Hotel," Smith replied, "masquerading as a member of his own suite."

He was silent for a moment, and, then:

"The first time I ever used a sandbag," he said reflectively, weighing one of those weapons in his hand. "But having actually reached Victoria without incident, I determined that *this* was the point of attack. A transfer of overcoats was made on the train, and the muffled gentleman who entered the Park Avenue was not Swâzi Pasha, but I! Multân Bey, the secretary, escaped at a suitable moment and left me in sole possession of Suite Number 5.

"I didn't know what to expect, but I was prepared for anything. And you must remember, Petrie,"—turning to the latter—"that I had had some little experience of the methods of this group! I heard the sound, faint though it was, high up in the ventilation shaft—the same which disturbed you, Greville. Then a hazy idea of what to expect dawned on my mind. A sandbag, the history of which I must tell you later, was in my trunk in the lobby. As I came out to secure it, since I considered it to be the most suitable instrument for my purpose, I heard your soft but rapid footsteps, Greville. I realized that *someone* was approaching the door; that he must be stopped knocking or ringing at all costs, since my purpose was to catch the enemy red-handed."

There was a pause, and then:

"It's very late," said Dr. Petrie slowly, his gaze set upon Nayland Smith; "but I think, Smith, you owe us some further explanation."

"I agree," Nayland Smith replied quietly.

§ 4

IT WAS a strange party which gathered in the small hours in Dr. Petrie's sitting room. Petrie's wife, curled up in a shadowy corner of the divan, seemed in her fragile beauty utterly apart from this murderous business which had brought us together. Yet I knew that in the past she had been intimately linked with the monstrous organization which again was stretching out gaunt hands to move pieces on the chessboard of the world. Weymouth, in an armchair, smoked in stolid silence. Petrie stood on on the hearthrug watching Nayland Smith. And I, seated by the writing table, listened to a terse, unemotional account of an experience such as few men have passed through. Nayland Smith, speaking rapidly and smoking all the time—striking many matches, for his pipe constantly went out—paced up and down the room.

"You have asked me, Petrie," he said, "to explain why I allowed you to believe that I was dead. The answer is this: I had learned during my investigations in Egypt that an inquirer who has no official existence possesses definite advantages. My dear fellow," —he turned impulsively to the doctor—"I knew it would hurt, but I knew there was a cure. Forgive me. The fate of millions was at stake. I will tell you the steps by which I arrived at this decision.

"I don't know how much you recall, Greville, of that

meeting at the house of the Sheikh Ismail. But you remember that I recognized the venerable mandarin who received us in the lobby? It was none other than Ki Ming, president of the Council of Seven! You remember the raid in London, Weymouth, and the diplomatic evasion by which he slipped through our fingers?"

"Very clearly," Weymouth replied.

"One of the finest brains and most formidable personalities in the world to-day. I rank him second only to Dr. Fu Manchu. I have yet to test the full strength of the lady known as 'Madame Ingomar,' but possibly she is deserving of a place. We shall see. I doubted if he knew me, Greville. Even had I been sure, I don't know what I could have done. But at least I knew my man and saw our danger."

"*I* had seen it all along," I interrupted.

Nayland Smith smiled, and:

"A. V. C. would not be too high a reward for your courage on that occasion!" he said. "Had the mandarin been sure, he would never have admitted us to the council. *He only suspected;* but he took instant steps to check these suspicions. I didn't like the way Sheikh Ismail looked at us when he came in.

"A messenger had been despatched to el-Khârga to make sure that the Tibetan deputies had actually set out. He found them on the way. They must have succeeded in attracting his attention. That messenger was the third member of the Burmese party—the Dacoit who was absent from the council.

"The two gong notes told me what had happened. As Ki Ming began to speak—denouncing us—I glanced back.

"That gigantic Negro door-keeper—he had entered and approached us silently as a cat—was in the act of throwing a silk scarf over your head! . . . the third Dacoit stood at my elbow.

"One's brain acts swiftly at such times. I realized that the mandarin's orders were that we be taken alive. But simultaneously, I realized that the Sheikh el-Jébal had his atrociously wicked eyes fixed upon me in an unmistakable way.

"These thoughts, these actions, occupied seconds. I

could not possibly save you. Resistance to such men and such numbers was out of the question. I could only hope to save myself and to rescue you by cunning.

Such a statement, spoken incisively, coolly, from another than Sir Denis Nayland Smith must have sounded equivocal. Coming from him, it sounded what it was—the considered decision of a master strategist.

"You remember our position, Greville? We weren't ten paces from the steps on the top of which Fah Lo Suee stood. Anticipating the intention of the Old Man of the Mountain and of the Burman who now sprang like a leopard, I ducked. He missed me . . . and I raced across the floor, up the steps, and before madame could realize my purpose, had one arm around her waist and the muzzle of a pistol tight against her ear!"

Nayland Smith paused for a moment, and we remained silent, spellbound, until:

"She is not human, that woman," came a hushed voice. "She is a vampire—she has *his* blood in her."

All eyes turned in the direction of the divan. Mrs. Petrie was the speaker.

"I agree with you," Nayland Smith replied coolly. "A human woman would have screamed, fought, or fainted. Fah Lo Suee merely smiled, and scornfully. Nevertheless I had won, for the moment. Her lips smiled, but her cold green eyes read the truth in mine.

"'Tell them,' I directed her, 'that if anyone stirs a finger I shall shoot you!'

"She continued to smile, and 'Please move your pistol,' she asked, 'so that I may speak.' I moved the pistol swiftly from her head to her heart. She looked aside at me and paid me a compliment which I shall always value: 'You are clever,' she said. Then she spoke to the petrified murderers in the room below.

"I risked one swift glance. . . . You had disappeared, Greville. The Negro had carried you out! . . . Fah Lo Suee began to speak. The cloak of her father has fallen upon her. She spoke as coolly as if I had not been present. First in Chinese, then in Hindustani, and thirdly in Arabic.

"Then: 'Order all to remain where they are,' I said —'except one, who is to give instructions for my friend to be brought to meet me outside the house.' She gave these orders—and the frustrated Dacoit, who still crouched on the mattress where he had fallen, went to carry out my directions.

" 'Lead the way!' I said.

"She turned, I knew I was safe for the moment. We entered a little room upon which the big doors opened. This room was not empty. . . . She was well guarded. And never can I forget her guards! Half a dozen words, however, reduced them to impotence. I could not afford to take my eyes off Fah Lo Suee for long; but nevertheless, as we passed through that anteroom, I solved a mystery. I grasped the explanation of something which has been puzzling us since it became evident that the first step in this new campaign of devilry was directed towards the Tomb of the Black Ape."

He paused, beginning to knock out his pipe, and:

"Yes, Sir Denis," I said eagerly, "go on!"

He turned to me smiling grimly.

"This is your particular province, Greville," he continued, "which fate brought into mine. It isn't any secret of the ancient Egyptians; it's something more dangerous —more useful. For in that room, Petrie," he turned now to the doctor—"were phials, instruments, and queer-looking yellow-bound books. Also several caskets, definitely of Chinese workmanship."

"I'm afraid I don't understand," Petrie confessed.

"Possibly I can enlighten you," said Nayland Smith, "for I think I have solved the mystery. At some time between his supposed death in 1917 and this year, Dr. Fu Manchu concealed there the essential secrets of his mastery of the Eastern world; the unique drugs, the unknown works dealing with their employment—and the powers, whether tangible—amulets and signets—or instructional and contained in his papers, which gave him control of practically all the fanatical sects of the East."

"Good God!" Weymouth murmured.

"This was what Dr. Fu Manchu's daughter went to

Egypt to recover. This was why Professor Zeitland was murdered. Barton escaped by a miracle. Their possession, you understand. . . ."

He paused in his restless promenade and looked about from face to face.

"Their possession made her mistress of the most formidable criminal organization in the world!"

§5

"I WALKED with Fah Lo Suee through that strange house, across a path to a garden at the back—not that through which we had entered—and out onto a narrow road bordering the wall on the side which faced the palm grove. This path was deserted.

"'Where is he?' I demanded.

"Fah Lo Suee smiled a mocking smile, and:

"'You must be patient,' she replied. 'They have to bring him a long way.'

"I pocketed my pistol and contented myself with keeping an arm around her. It was a natural gesture, but one for which I was to pay a high price, as I shall tell you."

"Two men appeared around the angle of the wall carrying a limp body. They hesitated, looking towards us. Madame raised her hand. They came on. . . . I saw you, Greville, lying on the sandy path at my feet, insensible.

"I continued to clutch Fah Lo Suee tightly, and now I reached for my pistol. I had detected one of the Negro bearers looking across my shoulder in a curiously significant way. . . ."

He paused and struck a match; then:

"It was short warning," he added, "but it might have been enough. If I had had the pistol against Fah Lo Suee's ribs, to-day the world would be rid of a very dangerous devil.

"Someone dropped from the wall behind me . . . and a swift blow with a sandbag concluded this episode!"

Nayland Smith raised his hand reflectively to his skull.

"I woke up amid complete silence, my head singing

like a kettle. I was slow to realize the facts; but when I did I was appalled. That lonely house is shunned by all, I have learned; for the Sheikh Ismail has an evil reputation as a dealer in Black Magic. I was a prisoner there. What were my chances?

"I was in a cell, Greville,"—he suddenly turned to me in the course of his ceaseless rambling walk—"some three yards square. I was lying on the hard mud floor. Not a thing had been taken from me; even my pistol remained in my belt . . . and the sandbag which had downed me lay close by! A subtle touch, that—But to-night I capped the jest! A window, just beyond reach, admitted light. There wasn't a scrap of furniture in the place. It had a heavy door reinforced with iron. I was desperately thirsty . . . and on the ledge of the window above me, I saw a water jar standing on a tray.

"Knowing myself to be in Egypt and failing my experience of Chinese humour, I might have questioned the meaning of all this. But, looking at the lock of the door, and taking out my pistol—to learn that the shells had been withdrawn—I knew. And I resigned myself.

"It was physically impossible to reach the water jar on the window ledge.

"I had been judged worthy of that Chinese penalty known as The Protracted Death. . . ."

§ 6

"PERHAPS I groaned when these facts forced themselves upon me. You see, Greville, as we entered the saloon I had recognized another undesirable acquaintance . . . Ibrahîm Bey—Swâzi's twin brother!

"I have known Swâzi Pasha for many years and in my newer capacity at Scotland Yard have had intimate dealings with him. Beyond doubt he stands between Turkey and that indeterminable menace some believe to emanate from Moscow and others from elsewhere—but which includes Turkey in its programme.

"Recognizing now the fact that Ibrahîm—a cold-blooded sedition monger—was a member of the Council of Seven, I knew! Here was the clue to those mysterious movements—of which you, Weymouth, had news, and which were painfully familiar to myself in the Near and Far East.

"Swâzi Pasha was doomed! . . . So, likewise, was I—the one man who might have saved him!

"You tell me, Weymouth, and you also, Petrie, that you searched the Sheikh's house from roof to cellar. One spot of cellar you overlooked—the spot in which *I* awakened!

"I had no means of knowing how long I had been unconscious. My wrist watch remained but had been smashed, doubtless as I fell. I had no means of learning if the raid had taken place. Two ideas were paramount. First, your fate, Greville. Second, Swâzi Pasha.

"I considered the window carefully. It was some two feet square, protected by rusty-looking iron bars, and from the nature of the light which it admitted, I determined that I was in a cellar and that the time was early morning. I determined, also, that the window was inaccessible. A careful examination of the door convinced me that I had no means of opening it. And since not a sound reached me, it was then I resigned myself to that most horrible of deaths—starvation and thirst . . . *Thirst*, with a moist jar of water standing on the ledge above me!

"From my condition I judged that only a few hours had elapsed, and I detected a sporting gesture on the part of Fah Lo Suee—a gamble characteristically Chinese. If anyone chanced to pass that way I might be rescued! All this was surmise, of course, but I decided to test it. My eyes were burning feverishly. My head throbbed madly. But otherwise I was vigorous enough. Loudly I cried for help in English and in Arabic. Then, I listened intently.

"There was no sound.

"A Buddhist-like resignation was threatening me more and more. But I was by no means disposed to abandon myself to it. To sit down was impossible, otherwise than on the floor—and I felt peculiarly limp. I leaned up against the door and weighed my chances.

"And it was at this moment that a good man announced his presence. Failing him, I shouldn't be here to-night!

"I heard the howl of a dog!

"*Said!*

"In that moment, Petrie,"—instinctively Nayland Smith turned to his old friend—"the face of the world changed for me! The mood of resignation passed. Standing immediately under the window, I howled a reply.

"The signal was repeated. I answered it. And two minutes later I heard Said's voice above.

"Details are unnecessary, now. He had to go back to the car for gear and a rope. Scrambling down the shallow well with which the window communicated, he succeeded in wrenching the bars loose.

"And so I climbed out, to find myself on the fringe of the palm grove. I can't blame you, Weymouth, for failing to discover this far-flung chamber of the Sheikh's house. Undoubtedly it had been designed for a dungeon. I can only suppose the iron-barred door communicated with a tunnel leading to the cellars.

"My mind was made up. Beneath my monkish cowl I was an Arab, and an Arab I would remain! I was heartsick about you, Greville, but knew that I could do nothing—yet. Stamboul was my objective. The reason you failed to find the car in the gully was that I commandeered it for the overland journey to the railroad!

"I had realized the efficiency of the organization to which I was opposed. My funds were fortunately sufficient for my purpose, and I reached Stamboul a week after the raid on the house of the Sheikh Ismail. Officially, I was not present in Constantinople. But I acquainted myself with the latest news in the possession of Scotland Yard—through the medium of Kemal's police. Acting upon this, I checked his journey in Paris. The rest you know."

Nayland Smith ceased speaking, and:

"Something you do *not* know," said Mrs. Petrie from her shadowy corner on the divan. "I have seen *him*—Fu Manchu, in London, to-night!"

Nayland Smith turned to her.

"You were never at fault, Karamanèh," he said. "Dr. Fu Manchu occupied rooms next to those of Swâzi Pasha in Paris!"

A taxi hooted outside in Piccadilly. . . .

PART FOUR

10 *ABBOTS HOLD*

"IT ALL seems so peaceful," said Rima, clinging very tightly to my arm; "yet somehow, Shan, I never feel safe here. Last night, as I told you, I thought I saw the Abbots Hold ghost from my window. . . ."

"A natural thing to imagine, darling," I replied reassuringly. "Every one of these old monastic houses has its phantom monk! But, even if authentic, no doubt he'd be a jovial fellow."

As is the fashion of such autumn disturbances, a storm which had been threatening all the evening hovered to the west, blackly. Remote peals of thunder there had been during dinner, and two short but heavy showers. Now, although angry cloud banks were visible in the distance, immediately overhead the sky was cloudless.

We sauntered on through the kitchen garden. A constant whispering in the trees told of moisture dripping from leaf to leaf. But the air was sweet and the path already dry. Rima's unrest was no matter for wonder, considering the experiences she had passed through. And when Sir Lionel had suggested our leaving London for the peace of his place in Norfolk, no one had welcomed the idea more heartily than I. In spite of intense activity on the part of Inspector Yale and his associates, all trace of Madame Ingomar—and of her yet more formidable father—had vanished.

But Nayland Smith considered that Sir Lionel, having

served Fah Lo Suee's purpose—might now be considered safe from molestation and we had settled down in Abbots Hold for a spell of rest.

"The queer thing is," Rima went on, a deep earnest note coming into her voice, "that since Sir Denis joined us I have felt not more but *less* secure!"

"That's very curious," I murmured, "because I've had an extraordinary feeling of the sort, myself."

"I suppose I'm very jumpy," Rima confessed, "But did you notice that family of gypsies who've camped beyond the plantation?"

"Yes, dear. I passed them to-day. I saw a boy—rather a good-looking boy he seemed to be, but I was some distance off—and an awful old hag of a woman. Do they worry you?"

Rima laughed, unnaturally.

"Not really. I haven't seen the boy. But the woman and man I met in the lane simply gave me the creeps—"

She broke off; then:

"Oh, Shan! what's that!" she whispered.

A deep purring sound came to my ears—continuous and strange. For a moment I stood still, whilst Rima's fingers clung close to mine. Then an explanation occurred to me

Not noticing our direction, we had reached the corner of a sort of out-house connected by a covered passage with part of the servants' quarters.

"You understand now, darling," I said, and drew Rima forward to an iron-barred window.

Bright moonlight made the interior visible; and coiled on the floor, his wicked little head raised to watch us, lay a graceful catlike creature whose black-spotted coat of gold gleamed through the dusk.

It was Sir Lionel's Indian cheetah—although fairly tame, at times a dangerous pet. Practical zoology had always been one of the chief's hobbies.

"Oh, thank heaven!" Rima exclaimed, looking down into the beautiful savage eyes which were raised to hers —"I might have guessed! But I never heard him purring before."

"He is evidently in a good humour," I said, as the

great cat, with what I suppose was a friendly snarl,
stood up with slow, feline grace, yawned, snarled again,
and seemed to collapse wearily on the floor. The idea
flashed through my mind that it was not a bad imitation of a drunken man!

This idea was even better than I realized at the time.

We walked on, round the west wing of the rambling
old building, and finally entered the library by way of
the French windows. Sir Lionel had certainly changed
the atmosphere of this room. The spacious apartment
with its oak-panelled walls and the great ceiling beams
displayed the influence of the Orientalist in the form of
numberless Eastern relics and curiosities, which seemed
strangely out of place. Memories of the cloister clung
more tenaciously here—the old refectory—than to any
other room in Abbots Hold.

A magnificent Chinese lacquer cabinet, fully six feet
high, which stood like a grotesque sentry box just below
the newel post of the staircase struck perhaps the most
blatant discord of all.

The library was empty, but I could hear the chief's
loud voice in the study upstairs, and I knew that Nayland Smith was there with him. Petrie and his wife had
been expected to dinner, but they had telephoned from
Norwich to notify us that they would be detained over-
night, owing to engine trouble.

Mrs. Oram, Sir Lionel's white-haired old housekeeper,
presently came in; and leaving her chatting with Rima,
I went up the open oak staircase and joined the chief in
his study.

"Hullo, old scout!" he greeted me as I entered. "If
you're going to work with *me* in future, you'll either
have to chuck Rima or marry her!"

He was standing on the hearth rug, dominating that
small room which was so laden with relics of his exten-
sive and unusual travels that it resembled the shop of a
very untidy antique dealer.

Nayland Smith, seated on a corner of the littered writing table, was tugging at the lobe of his left ear and
staring critically at the big brown-skinned man with his
untidy, gray-white hair and keen blue eyes who was

England's most intrepid explored and foremost Orientalist. It was a toss-up which of these two contained the more volcanic energy.

"Smith's worried," Sir Lionel went on in his loud, rapid manner. "He thinks our Chinese friends are up to their monkey tricks again and he doesn't like Petrie's delay."

"I don't," snapped Nayland Smith. "It may be an accident. But, coming to-night, I wonder—"

"Why *to-night?*" I asked.

Nayland Smith stared at me intently; then:

"Because to-night I caught a glimpse of the Abbots Hold ghost."

"Rot!" shouted Sir Lionel.

"The monk?" I asked excitedly.

Nayland Smith shook his head.

"No! Didn't look like a monk to me," he said.

"And I don't believe in ghosts!" he added.

§ 2

WHEN I rejoined Rima, her restless mood had grown more marked.

"I'm so glad you're here, Shan," she said. "Dear old Mrs. Oram has gone to bed; and although I could hear your voices in the study I felt quite ridiculously nervous. I'm terribly disappointed about the Petries."

During their short acquaintance Rima and Mrs. Petrie had established one of those rare feminine friendships which a man can welcome. In Mrs. Petrie's complex character there was a marked streak of Oriental mysticism—although from her appearance I should never have suspected Eastern blood; and Rima had that Celtic leaning towards a fairyland beyond the common ken which was part and parcel of her birthright.

"So am I, darling," I said. "But they'll be here in the morning. Have you been imagining things again?" I glanced at the French windows. "Peters has locked up, I see. So you can't have been nervous about gypsies!"

It was strange that Rima, who had shared our queer life out in the Valley of the Kings, should be so timorous in a Norfolk country house; should fear wandering gypsies who had never feared Bedouins!

"No." She looked at me in her serious way, apparently reading my thoughts. "I'm *not* afraid of gypsies—really. I have spent too many nights out there in the wâdi in Egypt to be afraid of anything like that. It is a sort of silly, *unreal* fear, Shan! Will you please do something?"

"Anything! What?"

Rima pointed to the Chinese cabinet at the foot of the stairs.

"Please open it!"

I crossed to the ornate piece of furniture and flung its gold-lined doors open. The cabinet was empty—as I had expected.

Rima thanked me with a smile, and:

"I've been fighting a horrible temptation to do just that," she confessed, "for a long time! Thank you, Shan dear. Don't think I'm mad but, truly,"—she held out the book she had had on her knees—"for ever so long past I have been sitting here reading and rereading this one line—and glancing sideways at the cabinet. You seemed to wake me out of a trance!"

I took the book—a modern novel—and glanced at the line upon which Rima's finger rested. It was:

"*I am near you . . .*"

"Could anything be more absurd?" she asked, pathetically. "What's wrong with me?" . . .

I could find no answer, then—except a lover's answer. But I was to learn later.

When at last we said good-night, I noticed as Rima stood up that she had a scent spray on the cushions beside her, and laughingly:

"What's the idea?" I asked.

She considered my question in an oddly serious way. In fact, her mood was distrait in an unusual degree; but finally:

"I had almost forgotten," she replied, with a faraway look; "but I remember, now, that there was a fusty smell, like decaying leaves. I thought a whiff of eau-de-Cologne would freshen the air."

My room was on the southwest front of Abbots Hold. It was one of those in the Georgian wing, and an ugly stone balcony stretched along before it. Beneath this balcony ran a sort of arcade behind which iron-barred windows belonging to the domestic quarters faced on sloping lawns. Above were these fine, spacious rooms reserved for guests, and the prospect was magnificent. Next to me was Nayland Smith; then there was a vacant room, and then Rima's.

On entering I did not turn up the light. There was a private plant in Abbots Hold installed by Sir Lionel. But, groping my way across, I raised the blind and looked out.

Opening the French window, I inhaled the fragrance of moist loam and newly wetted leaves. Away on the right I had a view of a corner of the terrace; directly before me the ground dropped steeply to a belt of trees bordering the former moat; beyond, it rose again, and two miles away, upstanding weirdly beyond distant park land, showed a ruined tower, one of the local landmarks, and a relic of Norman days.

At first my survey of the prospect was general and vague; indeed, I had opened the window more to enjoy the coolness of the night air and to think about Rima than for any other reason. But now, suddenly, my entire interest became focused upon the ruined tower rising ghostly above surrounding trees.

Clearly visible against a stormy backing, one little point of light high up in the tower appeared and disappeared like a winking eye!

I clenched my teeth, craning out and watching intently. A code message was being transmitted from the tower! For a while I watched it, but I had forgotten Morse, and the dots and dashes defeated me. Then came inspiration: someone in Abbots Hold must be receiving this message!

Instant upon the birth of the theory, I acted.

The geography of the neighbourhood, which I knew fairly well, told me that this message could only be intended for Abbots Hold. Neglectful of the fact that the leaves were drenched with rain, I quickly got astride of the ledge and began to climb down the ivy to the shrubbery beneath.

I dropped into wet bushes without other mishap

than the saturating of my dinner kit, and keeping well within the shadow of the house I began to work my way round in the direction of the terrace. I passed the dining room, glancing up at the rooms above it, and proceeded. The whole house was in darkness.

Below the terrace I paused, looking again toward the distant tower.

The top remained just visible above the trees . . . and there, still coming and going, was the signal light!

I stepped out farther from the building, cautiously, looking upward to the left.

"Ah!" I muttered.

Dropping down upon the sloping lawn, its turf still wet from the recent downpour, I crept farther northward, until I could obtain a clear view of the study window.

The room was in darkness, but the curtains were not drawn. A light, probably that of an electric torch, was coming and going, dot and dash, *in the chief's study!*

I came to the end of the terrace, and taking advantage of a bank of rhododendrons, crept farther away from the house, until I could see, not merely the reflection, but the actual light being operated.

Faintly as it glowed in the darkness, I could detect the figure of one who held it . . . And at first I was loath to credit what I saw.

The legend of Abbots Hold; Rima's fears; memories —dreadful memories—of my own, must certainly, I determined, be influencing my imagination.

The man signalling to that other on the distant tower —for a man I assumed the signaller to be—was wrapped in a sort of *cowl* . . . his head so enveloped in the huge hood that in the dim reflection of the torch it was quite impossible to detect his features.

"Good God!" I muttered. "What does this mean!"

Stooping below the level of the bushes, I turned. Regaining the shelter of the terrace, I ran for twenty paces. Then, leaping into the shrubbery, I located the thick branch of ivy which was a ladder to my window, and began to climb up again, my heart beating very fast, and my thoughts racing far ahead of physical effort.

Scrambling over the stone balustrade, I stepped towards the open French window of my room. . . .

Out of the shadows into the moonlight a figure moved. It was Nayland Smith!

§ 3

"Ssh! Speak quietly, Greville!"

I stared in amazement, standing there breathing heavily by the open window, then:

"Why?" I asked in a low voice. "What's happened?"

"Close the window," said Smith.

I obeyed, and then, turning:

"Did you see me climbing up?" I asked.

"No. I heard you. I was afraid to show myself. I was expecting someone else! But you are bursting with news. Tell me."

Quickly I told him of the light beyond the valley—of the cowled figure in the study.

"Too late to trap him now, Sir Denis!" I finished, starting for the door.

He grabbed my arm.

"Not too late!" he rapped. "Here he is!"

I threw a quick and startled glance around the room, as:

"Where?" I demanded.

"There!"

Nayland Smith pointed to my bed.

Amazed to the verge of losing control, I stared at the bed. A rough, camel-hair garment lay there . . . I moved, touched it. Then I knew.

"It's the robe of a Lama monk!"

Nayland Smith nodded grimly.

"Together with a certain sandbag," he said, "it has formed part of my baggage since that eventful meeting of the Council of Seven at el-Khârga!"

"But—"

"Why did I play ghost? Very simple. I suspected that some member of the household was in league with the enemy. I believe, now, I was wrong. But I knew that wherever my private inquiries led me, no one would challenge the hooded monk of Abbotts Hold!"

"Good enough," I admitted. "But you were signalling from the study!"

"I was!" Nayland Smith rapped. "I was signalling to Weymouth who was watching from the tower."

"To *Weymouth!*"

"Exactly! Weymouth reported in that way to me—as had been arranged; and I gave him certain instructions in return."

I looked him squarely in the face, and:

"Does the chief know that Superintendent Weymouth is standing by?" I asked.

"He does not!" Nayland Smith smiled, and my anger began to melt. "That rather takes the wind out of your angry sails, Greville!" He grasped my shoulder. "I don't trust Barton!" he added.

"What!"

"I don't trust *you*. . . Both have been under the influence of Fah Lo Suee. And to-night I don't trust Rima!"

I had dropped down onto the bed, but now I started up. Into the sudden silence, like the growling of angry beasts, came an echo of thunder away eastward.

"What the devil do you mean?"

"Ssh!" Nayland Smith restrained me; his gaze was compelling. "You heard me say to-night that I had had my first glimpse of the ghost?"

"Well?"

"It was true. The 'ghost' slipped through my fingers. But the ghost was *Fah Lo Suee!* . . . Don't raise your voice. I have a reason for this. Just outline to me, without any reservation, what took place from the time that you left Barton's study to the time that you said good-night to Rima."

I stared blankly for a moment, then:

"You are her accepted lover," he added, "and she is very charming. I congratulate you . . . and give you my permission to leave out the kisses. . . ."

§ 4

"RIMA was obsessed with the idea," I said, "that someone was hiding in the big lacquer cabinet. But her frame of mind seems to have been such that she wouldn't stoop to test this suspicion."

"Very characteristic," Nayland Smith commented. "You may remember that I left Barton's study some time ahead of you?"

"Yes."

"The cabinet in question stands beside the newel post of the staircase, and as the library was lighted to-night, in deep shadow. It has certain properties, Greville, with which I am acquainted but which may be unfamiliar to you. It's a very old piece and I had examined it in the past. It has lacquered doors in front and a plain door at the back!"

"Do you mean—"

"Precisely! As I came out of the study, I noticed a curious passivity in Rima's attitude which aroused my interest. Also, she was not reading, as your account would lead one to suppose—but, twisted around in her chair, was staring rigidly at the French windows! The staircase, you remember, is not visible from outside!"

"Then—"

"Her suspicion—which came later—was based on fact. *I* was in the cabinet!"

"But when—"

"Did I withdraw? Husband your blushes. I escaped at the moment you entered the room, and slipped unnoticed through the door leading to the servants' quarters below the staircase. I made my way back to the study *via* the east wing, and waited for Weymouth's signal. I had another small problem to investigate en route and so I grabbed my useful ghostly disguise!"

"What was the small problem?"

"The cheetah!"

"The cheetah?"

"A tame cheetah, Greville, is more sensitive than any ordinary domestic animal to the presence of *strangers*. He is used to Barton's guests, but an intruder would provoke howls calculated to rouse the house. I suspected that the cat had been doped."

"By heaven, you're right!"

"I know I'm right! When I went round there in my

monkish disguise he was snoring like an elephant! But please go on."

To the best of my ability I outlined what Rima had told me of her mood of passive terror. I tried to explain that I had reassured her and had finally parted from her confident that she was restored to normal; but:

"There's something wrong," Nayland Smith rapped irritably; "and time is important. She went out of the library—I'll swear, to fetch something—just before you came in—and she opened and then reclosed the windows."

"I'm sorry!" I exclaimed.

"Ssh!"

"I had overlooked it, Sir Denis—although it isn't of the slightest importance. She had gone to her room to get a scent-spray containing eau-de-Cologne."

Nayland Smith, who had been walking across and across the rug beside the bed, pulled up with a jerk.

"Not of the slightest importance? It's what I've been waiting to hear! At last I understand the strong smell of eau-de-Cologne which I detected on the terrace outside the library. . . Quick! *You* are privileged. . . . Steal along to Rima's room. Take your shoes off. Go by the balcony. Her window is open, no doubt. If she's awake —which I think unlikely—ask her for the eau-de-Cologne bottle. Explain things how you like. If she's asleep, find it—and bring it to me! Take this torch. . . ."

§ 5

THE STRANGE theft was accomplished without a hitch. Rima slept soundly. Although her dressing table was littered with bottles, I found the spray easily enough— for it was the only one of its kind there. I hurried back to my room.

Nayland Smith took it from my hands as though it had been a live bomb. He opened the door and went out. I heard him turn a tap on in the bathroom. Then he returned—carrying the spray. I saw that it was still half full.

"Take it back," he directed.

And I replaced it on Rima's dressing table without arousing her.

"Good," Smith acknowledged. "Now we enter a province of surmise."

He began to pace the mat again, deep in thought; then:

"*I* am the likeliest!" he snapped suddenly; and although I couldn't imagine what he meant, went on immediately: "Conceal yourself in the south corner of the balcony. The ivy is thick there. Keep your shoes off. We must be silent."

As the paving was still wet, my prospect was poor; but:

"If anyone moves in Rima's room," he continued rapidly, "don't stir. If anyone comes out onto the balcony —watch. But whoever it is, do nothing. Just watch. If necessary, follow, but don't speak and don't be discovered. Off you go, Greville!"

I had already started, when:

"It may be a bit of an ordeal," he added, "but I count on you."

Past the open window of Smith's room I went and past that, closed, which belonged to the vacant room. Then, creeping silently, I went by Rima's window and crouched down among a tangle of wet ivy in the corner formed by the stone balustrade.

The sky directly above was cloudless again, and part of the balcony gleamed phantomesque in silvery moonlight. But, another part, including the corner in which I lay concealed, was in deep shadow. From somewhere a long way off—perhaps over the sea—came dim drumming of thunder. About me whispered leaves of rain-drenched foliage.

I saw Nayland Smith go into his room.

What were we waiting for?

Abbots Hold was silent. Nothing stirred, until a soft fluttering immediately above me set my heart thumping.

An owl swept out from the eaves and disappeared in the direction of the big plantation. From some reed bed of the near-by river a disturbed lapwing gave her eerie, *peewit* cry. The cry was repeated; then answered far away. Silence fell once more.

My post was a cold and uncomfortable one. It was characteristic of Nayland Smith that he took no count of such details where either himself or another was concerned. The job in hand overrode in importance any such trivial considerations.

Presently I heard the big library clock strike—and I counted the strokes mechanically.

Midnight.

I reflected that in London, now, folk would just be finishing supper.

Then . . . *I saw her!*

I suppose—I hope—I shall never again experience just the sort of shock which gripped my heart at this moment. Vaguely, I had imagined that our purpose was protective; that I was on guard because Rima's safety was at stake in some way. To the mystery of Nayland Smith's words, "*I* am the likeliest," I had failed all along to discover any solution.

Now, the solution came . . . hazily at first.

Rima, a fairy gossamer figure in the moonlight, came out barefooted onto the terrace!

Unhesitatingly, she turned right, passed the vacant room and entered the open window of that occupied by Nayland Smith! I could not believe the evidence of my senses. Just in the nick of time I checked her name as it leaped to my lips.

" . . . You must be silent. It may be a bit of an ordeal —but I count on you. . . ."

Rising slowly to my feet, I stole along the terrace. The moon shone into Smith's room as it shone into mine. Just before reaching the window, I dropped down on my knees and cautiously craned forward to peer in.

Nayland Smith was in bed, the sheets drawn up to his chin. His eyes were closed . . . and Rima stood beside him.

Something that had puzzled me in that first stunning moment now resolved itself—grotesquely. I had realized that Rima carried a glittering object. I saw it clearly as I peered into the room.

It was the scent spray!

And, as I watched, I saw her stoop and spray the face of the motionless man in the bed!

She turned. . . . She was coming out again.

I drew back and hurried to my shadowy corner. Rima appeared in the moonlight. She looked unnaturally pale. But with never a glance to right or left she walked to her room and went in. Her eyes were wide open—staring.

Absolute silence. . . .

Then Nayland Smith appeared. He was fully dressed but he had removed his shoes.

He signalled to me to approach Rima's window. A man stupefied—horror, amazement, incredulity, each fighting for a place—I obeyed. Dropping to my knees again, I peered in. . . .

Rima, at the green marble wash-basin, was emptying the scent spray! She allowed hot water to run for some time, and then carefully rinsed the container and the fitting. Replacing the latter in position, she put the bottle on the dressing table where I had found it . . . and went to bed!

Nayland Smith beckoned to me. I rose and walked very unsteadily along the terrace to his room.

§ 6

"RIMA!" I said. "*Rima!* My God, Sir Denis, what does it mean?"

He grasped my shoulder hard.

"Nothing," he replied.

His keen eyes studied my amazement.

"Nothing?"

"Just that—nothing. I warned you it might prove to be an ordeal. Sit down. A peg of whisky will do us both good. . . ."

I sat down without another word. And Nayland Smith brewed two stiff pegs. Handing one to me:

"Here's part of the explanation," he jerked—and held a book under my nose. "Smell. Only *one* sniff!"

A sickly-sweet odour came from the open pages. The book was that which Rima had been reading in the library.

"Familiar?"

I nodded; and took a long drink. My hand was none too steady. It was a perfume I could never forget. It formed my last memory of the meeting of the Seven at el-Khârga; my first memory of that dreadful awakening in the green-gold room in Limehouse!

"*Hashîsh!*" snapped Nayland Smith— "or something prepared from it. Rima, by means of this doped book, was put into a *receptive* condition. It's a routine, Greville, with which Petrie is unhappily familiar . . . hence Petrie's detention on the way!

"Fah Lo Suee is an accomplished *hypnotist!* For this piece of information I am also indebted to the doctor: he once all but succumbed to her . . . and she was only in her teens in those days. She was posted outside the closed French windows of the library tonight. In some way, and at the psychological moment, she attracted Rima's attention—and obtained mental control over her."

"But . . . is this possible?"

"You have seen it in full operation," he answered. "Rima was given hypnotic orders to go to her room for a scent spray. She obeyed. That was when from my post in the Chinese cabinet I heard her hurry upstairs. She brought the spray, opened the window—I heard her —and gave it to Fah Lo Suee (whose name, by the way, means 'Sweet Perfume'). It was emptied, recharged and returned to her. She reclosed the window . . . having received those detailed post-hypnotic instructions which we have seen her carry out to-night."

"But"—my bewilderment was increasing—"I *spoke* to her after this! I even asked her why she had fetched the scent spray, and she said she had detected a sickly smell —like decaying leaves—and thought it would freshen the air."

"Part of her orders!" he rapped. "Next, she was instructed to go to bed and sleep until midnight; then to spray *me* with the contents (which I preserved for analysis and replaced with water!) and then to remove all traces—as we know she did do! My dear fellow, Rima is utterly unaware that she has played this part . . . and doubtless it would have been an easy death!"

"You mean, when she wakes, she will know nothing about it?"

"Nothing whatever! Unless, perhaps, as in Petrie's case, the memory of a troubled dream. However, I have hopes . . . if my Morse orders were promptly obeyed."

"You mean your signal to Weymouth?"

He nodded, and:

"The 'gypsies'," he rapped.

"What!"

"Three are Dacoits—one posing as an old hag! The 'boy' of the party is Fah Lo Suee!"

11 DR. AMBER

"I CAN'T blame myself," said Weymouth, staring disconsolately out of the window. "She's slipped through our fingers again. A real chip of the old block," he added. "It took a load off my mind, after the Limehouse raid, to hear that Nayland Smith had seen *the Doctor,* in person, in Paris—and lost him! . . ."

The "gypsy" caravan behind the big plantation which formed a western boundary to Sir Lionel's Norfolk place had been seized by a party of constabulary under Weymouth's command—and had proved to be empty. This had happened three days before, but it still rankled in the superintendent's mind.

"I can't hang on here indefinitely," he explained. "I'm badly needed in Cairo at the moment. The disappearance of Sir Denis and yourself was the real excuse for my leave, but now . . ."

His point was clear enough. Weymouth was a staunch friend, but he loved his job. He had come to England in pursuit of a clue which suggested that Nayland Smith and I had been smuggled into Europe. We were found. Duty called him back.

"It isn't your present job, I admit," said I; "but it's the tail end of an old one, after all!"

He turned and stared at me across the room. I was back at the Park Avenue looking after a hundred and one interests of the chief's which centred in London. He, with Rima, remained in Norfolk—where, now that Nayland Smith had left, he might count on peace. Of Nayland Smith's present movements I knew nothing.

"You've hit it!" Weymouth admitted. "I'd like to be in at the death."

Certainly it was a queer situation for him—for all of us. Dr. Fu Manchu, most formidable of all those greater criminals who from time to time disturb the world, was alive . . . and his daughter, no poor second to this stupendous genius, had already proved that she was competent to form the subject of debate in the counsels of the highest.

Weymouth's expression struck me as ominous; and:

"The death is likely to be that of Nayland Smith," I said, "judging from our experience at Abbots Hold."

Weymouth nodded.

"He stands between her and all she aims for," he replied. "He's countered two of her best three moves and he's promised me word within the next hour. But"—he stared at me very grimly—"you and I, Greville, know more about the group called the *Si Fan* than most people outside it."

I laughed—somewhat hollowly, perhaps.

"Get back to Cairo," I advised. "It's probably safer than London at the moment—for you."

Weymouth's sense of humour on such points always failed him. His blue eyes hardened; he literally glared at me; and:

"I never ran away from Dr. Fu Manchu," he replied. "If you think I'm going to run away from his daughter you're wrong."

At that I laughed again, and this time, my laughter rang true. I punched the speaker playfully.

"Don't you know when I'm pulling your leg?" I asked. "I'd put my last shilling on your being here, job or no job, until the end of this thing is clearly in sight!"

"Oh!" said Weymouth, his naive smile softening the hard mask which had fallen when I had suggested his retiring to Cairo. "Well, I don't think you'd lose your money."

But when he had gone, I took his place at the window and stared down on the panorama of Piccadilly. I was thinking of Nayland Smith. . . . "He stands between her and all she aims for." . . . How true that was! Yes, he held most of the strings. Fah Lo Suee had started with a heavy handicap. Ibrahîm Bey occupied a cell in Brixton Prison. He would be tried and duly sentenced for attempted robbery with violence. The public would never learn the whole truth. But Ibrahîm Bey might be counted out of the running. The Egyptian authorities, working in concert with the French in Syria, were looking for Sheikh Ismail; and the Mandarin Ki Ming would have to hide very cleverly to escape the vigilance of those who had been advised of his aims. . . .

My phone bell rang. I turned and took up the receiver. "Yes?"

"Is Mr. Shan Greville there?"

"Speaking."

The voice—that of a man who spoke perfect English but was not an Englishman—sounded tauntingly familiar.

"My name will be known to you, I believe, Mr. Greville. I am called Dr. Amber."

Dr. Amber! The mysterious physician whose treatment had restored Sir Lionel—whom I had to thank for my own recovery!

"Owing to peculiar circumstances, which I hope to explain to you, I have hitherto been able to help only in a rather irregular way," he went on. "Because of this—and of the imminent danger to which I am exposed—I must make a somewhat odd request."

"What is it?"

"It is this: All I have to tell you is at your disposal. But you must promise to treat myself as non-existent. I have approached you in this way because the life of Sir Denis Nayland Smith is threatened—to-night! My record backs my assurance that this is a friendly overture. Have I your promise?"

"Yes—certainly!"

"Good. It will be a short journey, Mr. Greville,—not three minutes' walk. I am staying at Babylon House, Piccadilly; Flat Number 7. May I ask you to step across? You have ample time before dinner."

"I'll come right away."

Dr. Amber! Who was Dr. Amber? Where did he fit into this intricate puzzle which had sidetracked so many lives? Whoever he might be, he had shown himself a friend, and without hesitation, but fired by an intense curiosity, I set out for Babylon House—a block of service flats nearly opposite Burlington Arcade.

A lift-man took me to the top floor and indicated a door on the right. I stepped up to it and rang the bell.

The elevator was already descending before the door opened . . . and I saw before me the Chinese physician who had attended me in that green and gold room in Limehouse!

Fear—incredulity—anger—all must have been readable in my expression, when:

"You gave me your promise, Mr. Greville," said the Chinaman, smiling. "I give you mine, if it is necessary, that you are safe and with a friend. Please come in."

§ 2

THE TYPICAL and scanty appointments of the apartment into which I was shown possessed a reassuring quality. From a high window with a narrow balcony I could see the entrance to Burlington Arcade and part of one wall of the Albany.

"Won't you sit down?" said my host, who wore morning dress and looked less characteristically Chinese than he had looked in white overalls.

I sat down.

A small writing desk set before the window was littered with torn documents, and a longer table in the centre of the room bore stacks of newspapers. I saw the London *Evening News*, the *Times of India*, and the Chicago *Tribune* amongst this odd assortment. Certain paragraphs appeared to have been cut out with scissors. The floor was littered with oddments. I noticed other definite evidences of a speedy outgoing. A very large steamer trunk bearing the initials L. K. S. in white letters stood strapped in a corner of the room.

"It is my purpose, Mr. Greville," said Dr. Amber, taking a seat near the desk and watching me steadily, "to explain certain matters which have been puzzling yourself and your friends. And perhaps in the first place, since I wish to be perf tly frank"—he glanced toward the big trunk—"I should tell you that 'Dr. Amber' is a pseudonym. I am called Li King Su; I hold a medical degree of Canton; and I once had the pleasure of assisting Dr. Petrie in a very critical major operation. He will probably remember me.

"You are quite naturally labouring under the impression that I belong to the organization controlled by the Lady Fah Lo Sue . This is not so. I belong to another, *older*, organization. . . ."

He stared at me intently. But I didn't interrupt him. I was considering that curious expression—"the Lady Fah Lo Suee."

"I was—shall we say?—a spy in the house in which you first met me. The lady called Fah Lo Suee has now discovered the imposture, and—"

Again he paused, indicating the steamer trunk.

"My usefulness is ended. I am a marked man, Mr. Greville. If I escape alive I shall be lucky. But let us talk of something else. . . . The Tomb of the Black Ape has proved something of a puzzle to Sir Denis Nayland Smith. The solution is simple: A representative of that older organization to which I have referred was present when Lafleur opened the place many years ago. By arrangement with that distinguished Egyptologist, it was reclosed. Later—in fact, early in 1918—a prominent official of our ancient society, passing through Egypt, had reason to suspect that certain treasures in his possession might be discovered and detained by the British authorities—for these were troubled times. He proceeded up the Nile and successfully concealed them in this tomb—

the secret of which had been preserved with just such an end in view...."

I suppose I must have known all along; but for some reason at this moment the identity of "a representative of that older organization" and "a prominent official of our ancient society" suddenly burst upon me with all the shock of novelty; and, meeting the glance of those inscrutable eyes which watched me so intently:

"You are speaking of *Dr. Fu Manchu!*" I said.

Li King Su permitted himself a slight deprecatory gesture.

"It is desirable," he replied, "that those of whom I speak should remain anonymous!"

But I continued to stare at him with a sort of horror. "By arrangement with that distinguished Egyptologist," he had said smoothly—

(Good God! What kind of "arrangement"!)—"it was the intention of the hider," he went on, "that these potent secrets should remain concealed for ever. The activities of Professor Zeitland and Sir Lionel Barton created an unforeseen situation. It was complicated by the action of the Lady Fah Lo Suee. She had recently learned what was hidden there, but she was ignorant of how to recover it.... Professor Zeitland imparted his knowledge to her—then came Sir Lionel Barton...."

He paused again, significantly.

"We moved too late, Mr. Greville. An old schism in our ranks had made an enemy of one of the most brilliant and dangerous men in China—the exalted Mandarin Ki Ming. He gave the Lady Fah Lo Suee his aid. But we wasted no more time. I succeeded in gaining admittance to their councils. It was by means of their organization that I intercepted Dr. Petrie's telegram to Sir Brian Hawkins. You know the use which I made of my knowledge.

"Your present English Government is blind. You will lose Egypt; you have lost India. A great federation of Eastern States affiliated with Russia—a new Russia—is destined to take the place once held by the British Empire. You have one chance to recover ..."

The man's personality was beginning to get me. I had

forgotten that I sat inert, listening to a self-confessed servant of Dr. Fu Manchu: I only knew that he was raising
veils beyond which I longed to peer.

"What is it?" I asked.

And, as I spoke, a chill—not figurative but literal—
turned me cold. I had detected Li King Su in the act of
glancing toward a partially opened door which led to
the bedroom. . . .

Definitely, *someone* was listening!

As if conscious of the fact that he had betrayed himself, "Dr. Amber" went on immediately:

"A counter alliance! But we are getting out of our
depth, Mr. Greville. To return to more personal matters: The schemes of the Lady Fah Lo Suee were not
approved by us. The authority she has stolen must be
restored to those who know how to wield it. In other
words, Sir Denis Nayland Smith's aims and our own
are identical—at the moment. But he is marked down!"

"He knows it!"

"He may know it—but to-night he is walking into a
trap! Since he left Norfolk—where he failed to arrest the
prime mover—you have lost touch with him. He is following up a clue discovered by Inspector Yale. It is a
false clue . . . a snare. He stands in the way: she is afraid
to move until he is silenced.

"Here"—he handed me a slip of paper—"is the address
to which he is going to-night. Death waits for him."

I glanced at the writing.

"The garden of this house adjoins the Regent Canal,"
Li King Su went on. "And it is intended that Sir Denis's
body shall be found in the Canal in the morning! Here"—
he passed a second slip—"is the address at which Sir
Denis is hiding."

The second address was that of a Dr. Murray in a
southwest suburb.

"Dr. Murray bought Dr. Petrie's practice," the even
voice continued, "when the latter went to Egypt. I must
warn you against any attempt to communicate by telephone. The Lady Fah Lo Suee has a spy in the house!
Take what steps you please, Mr. Greville, but move

quickly! For my own part, I leave London in an hour. I can do no more. It is unnecessary to remind you of our bargain."

§ 3

AT THE very moment that I entered the lift, that occult knowledge of *being watched* left me. It was the same—but intensified—as that which had warned me in Cairo, and later on the road to el-Khârga. Li King Su, on acquaintance, was a remarkable man. But some vastly greater personality had been concealed in that inner room. I could not forget that *Dr. Fu Manchu* had been seen a stone's throw from Babylon House!

Could I trust Li King Su?

Simple enough to test his statements. I had only to take a taxi to Dr. Murray's address.

But, I thought, as I walked out into Piccadilly, a mistake now might carry unimaginable consequences; better to consult Weymouth or Yale before I committed an irreparable blunder.

Dusk was falling. I saw that the lamps in Burlington Arcade had been lighted as well as those in the Piccadilly Arcade which forms a sort of abbreviated continuation of the older bazaar and breaks through to Jermyn Street. Deep in thought I passed the entrance to the latter. A French sedan was drawn up beside the pavement.

I was level with it when an exclamation of annoyance checked me sharply—and just prevented my collision with a woman who, crossing before me, had evidently been making for the car.

She was a fashionable figure, wearing a fur-trimmed coat, and a short veil attached to her close-fitting hat quite obscured her features. She carried several parcels, one of which she had dropped almost at my feet.

Stooping, I picked it up—a paper-wrapped package fastened with green tape and apparently containing very light purchases. The chauffeur sprang down and opened the door of the car, as:

"Thank you very much," said the laden lady. "Will you be so kind as to hand it in to me?"

She entered the car. I followed with the dropped package and bent forward into the dark interior. Through the opposite windows I saw the sign above a popular restaurant suddenly become illuminated. I detected a damnably familiar perfume . . .

I was enveloped. I felt a sudden paralyzing pressure in my spine—a muscular arm levered me into the car . . . and I realized that I had been garroted in Piccadilly, amid hundreds of passers-by and in sight of my hotel!

§4

I SHOT up from green depths in which I had been submerged for an immeasurable time. I had dived into a deep lake, I thought, and had become entangled in clinging weeds which sprang from its bed. I could not free my limbs; I knew that I was drowning—that never again should I see the sun and the blue sky above. . . .

Then, the clasp of those octopus tentacles was relaxed. And I shot to the surface like a cork. . . .

Green! . . . Everything about me was green!

What had happened? Where was I?

Great heavens! I was back in Limehouse! . . . But, no—this place was green and gold, but smaller—much smaller than the room of my long captivity.

It was a miniature room—something was radically wrong about it. There were two windows, draped in those heavy gold curtains which I remembered; a tracing of green figures was brushed across the gold. There was a tall lacquer cabinet and upon it stood a jade image of Kâli . . . tiny, minute. There were flat green doors and a green carpet; golden rugs. An amber lamp gave light. Upon a black divan was a second, larger figure of Kâli . . . as large as a carnival doll.

But, no! This figure resembled Kâli only in her features: she wore a green robe and high-heeled black shoes. In one slender hand, a soft hand nurtured in luxury, was a long cigarette holder. I could see the smoke from the burning cigarette. . . . A doll—but a living doll!

The picture grew smaller yet. The doll became so tiny that I could no longer discern her features. I was a giant in a microscopic room!

And then—the colours became *audible!*

"I am green," said the carpet. "We are gold," the miniature curtains replied. . . .

Raising both hands I clutched my head!

I was *mad!* I knew it—because I wanted to *laugh!*

The room began to increase in size! From the dimensions of a doll's house fashioned by gnomes it swelled to those of a gigantic palace! . . . I was a mere fly in an apartment which could scarcely have found ground space in Trafalgar Square!

But, now—I recognized that green-draped figure on the black divan. It was *Fah Lo Suee!*

The mighty roof, higher than that of any mosque, of any cathedral in the world, began to descend: the walls closed in . . . huge pieces of furniture were pushed towards me. Fah Lo Suee towered above my shrinking body, her monstrous cigarette sending up a column of smoke like that of a sacrifice. . . .

I cried out . . . and *saw the cry!*

"God help me!"

It issued from my lips in squat green letters! I closed my eyes, and:

"So you are awake, Shan?" said a bell-like voice.

But I was afraid to raise my eyelids.

"Look at me. You are all right now. . . ."

I looked.

My head was swimming and every muscle in my body ached—but the room had taken on normal proportions. It was a large room, filled with modern furniture, except that its scheme was severely green and gold and that there were Oriental pieces placed about.

Fah Lo Suee watched me . . . but the jade-green eyes were hard.

"You are better," she continued. "*Cannabis indica* produces strange delusions—but, as *we* use it, there is no drug so swift to serve our purpose."

I considered the situation. I was seated in a big armchair facing the divan upon which Fah Lo Suee reclined indolently watching me. The damnable fumes of the drug began to leave my brain. Fah Lo Suee, slender, sinuous, insolent, was a woman—but a deadly enemy. I knew what Nayland Smith would have done!

Preparatory to a spring, I drew my feet together . . . a certain distance. Then—

My ankles were fastened to the chair!

Fah Lo Suee dropped ash from her yellow cigarette into a copper bowl upon the low table beside her. I watched the elegant, voluptuous movements of that feline hand with a queer sense of novelty. What a tigress she was!

"The chief purpose of my visit to England," she said, speaking as though nothing unusual existed between hostess and visitor, "was defeated by Sir Denis Nayland Smith. My further plans are in abeyance—pending his removal."

My head ached as though my brain were on fire, but:

"He is by way of being rather a nuisance?" I suggested viciously.

Fah Lo Suee smiled, a smile of contempt.

"I could have dealt with him—alone. But one of my own people proved treacherous. In your pocket, Shan, you had two addresses. One was that of Dr. Murray—in whose home your brilliant friend is hiding; the other was that of this house."

She continued to smile—and she continued to watch me. I tried to conquer my wandering ideas. I tried to *hate* her. But her eyes caressed me, and I was afraid—horribly afraid of this witch-woman who had the uncanny power which Homer gave to Circe, of stealing men's souls.

If I could trust Li King Su, Nayland Smith was coming here—to this house—where death awaited!

And now I was powerless to stop him!

"Li King Su was a traitor." Through the beats of a sort of drumming which had started in my brain I heard the bell-like voice. "No doubt he counted on a great reward."

She ceased speaking and clapped her hands sharply.

That gigantic Negro who had been the door-keeper in el-Khârga, and who had overpowered me at the meeting of the Seven, came in!

Fah Lo Suee addressed him rapidly. She spoke in a sort of bastard Arabic—the Nubian dialect; and I found time for wonder. I knew North Africa from the inside; but I had never learned that queer lingo of the Nubians. Yet this woman—who was Chinese—used it familiarly!

The Nubian went out. Fah Lo Suee removed the stump of a yellow cigarette from her long holder, selected a fresh one from a cloisonné box, and fitted it into place. She ignited it with an enamelled lighter.

A dragging sound came.

I saw the Nubian pulling a heavy trunk through the door and across the carpet. This trunk was vaguely familiar. Then, on the top, I saw white painted initials: L.K.S.

The Negro removed the straps and threw the lid back.

"Look," said Fah Lo Suee. "He was a traitor."

Li King Su lay in his own trunk—dead!

§ 5

Not until I found myself alone could I think my own thoughts, uninfluenced by the promptings of those jade-green eyes. But when the door closed behind Fah Lo Suee, I began desperately to weigh my chances.

Nayland Smith was doomed!

This was the thought which came uppermost in my mind. The clue upon which he was working, and which would lead him that night to this house, was a false clue —a bait!

And that our enemies did not spare those who crossed their path I had learned.

The trunk had been dragged from the room. . . . But I could still see, in imagination, that strangled grin on the dead man's face.

I tried to reconstruct the details of our interview in Babylon House. Had I detected, or only deluded myself that I had detected, a swift exchange of signs between Li King Su and someone concealed in an inner room? Had I merely *imagined* the presence of this other? . . . Or had I been right in supposing someone to be there but wrong in my natural deduction that he was a friend of the Chinese doctor?

Had the hidden man murdered Li King Su and caused his body to be removed in the big trunk? . . .

"The garden of this house adjoins the Regent Canal," he had said.

The Regent Canal! A gloomy whispering waterway, now little used, and entering a long tunnel somewhere near this very spot where I found myself a prisoner!

I bent forward to inspect the fastenings which confined my ankles. . . . I was checked.

In the mad fantasies attendant upon my recovering from the effects of *hashish*, and afterwards under the evil thrall of Fah Lo Suee, I had failed to note a significant fact.

A rope was around my waist, binding me to the heavy chair!

True, my hands were free, but I could neither reach my ankles nor the knots fastening the line about my body, which were somewhere under the back of the chair.

A coffee table on which were whisky and soda and cigarettes stood conveniently near. I was about to take a cigarette . . . when I hesitated. Reaching to my pocket I took out my own case and with a lighter which lay on the table started a cigarette.

At all costs I must keep my head. Upon me, alone, rested the fate of Nayland Smith—perhaps the fate of a million more!

I smoked awhile, sitting deliberately relaxed, and thinking . . . thinking. My bonds occasioned me no inconvenience provided I remained inactive. Short of a painful, tortoise-like progress across the room, dragging the heavy chair with me, it became increasingly clear that to move was a physical impossibility.

The house was silent—very silent. Those heavy gold draperies seemed to exclude all sound.

For a long time I sat there, smoking cigarette after cigarette. Then I heard something.

One of the two doors opened.

The huge Nubian came in, carrying a tray upon which were sandwiches and fruit. He set the tray on the table beside me. His girth of shoulder was amazing; and as he stooped he gave me a wicked glance of his small, sunken, bloodshot eyes.

Without a word, he went out again, quietly closing the door.

Was I being watched? Having avoided the cigarettes and the whisky, was this a further attempt to dope me? I considered the facts. . . .

What had they to gain? I was utterly at their mercy. *Secret* poisoning was unnecessary.

I ate a sandwich and drank a glass of whisky and soda. Silence. . . .

The figure of Kâli on the lacquer cabinet engaged my attention. I found myself studying it closely—so closely that I began to imagine it was moving. . . .

Kâli—symbol of this hellish organization, the *Si Fan* into whose power I had fallen. . . .

The door opened, and Fah Lo Suee came in.

"I am glad to see that you have called on your philosophy," she said. "You will need it. Unless you are prepared to face another injection of *F.Katalepsis*, you must give me your parole for half an hour. . . ."

She stood in the open doorway, one slender hand, its polished nails gleaming like gems, resting on her hip. Her eyes were mercilessly hard.

I can't say what it was in her bearing that told me; but I knew, beyond any shadow of doubt, that all was not going smoothly with Madame Ingomar.

"Naturally, I must decline."

"You mean it?"

"Definitely."

She smiled. Her passionate lips betrayed a weakness which was not to be read in those jade-green eyes. She clapped her hands. The big emerald which she wore on an index finger glittered evilly.

The huge Nubian entered. Fah Lo Suee spoke rapidly, and he crossed to me.

"Don't resist," she said softly. "It would be merely melodrama. He could strangle you with one hand. Do as I ask. I am being merciful."

My wrists were firmly knotted behind me. Those lashings which held me to the heavy chair were cast off. Then the black picked me up as one might raise a child and carried me out of the room!

"In half an hour," said Fah Lo Suee, "I will free you again—and we will talk."

Clenching my teeth grimly—for curses, execrations, torrents of poisonous, futile words, bubbled up in me—I was borne across an elegantly furnished lobby. Everywhere I detected an ultra-modern note, in spite of the presence of old Oriental pieces.

Upstairs I was carried, and into a dark little room opening off the first floor landing. I was laid down, prone, on a narrow settee. The Nubian went out and locked the door. . . .

Trussed as I found myself, it was no easy matter to regain my feet. But I managed it, and stood staring around me in semi-darkness. The only light, I saw, came through a window which, on the outside, was reinforced with iron bars. And this light was the light of the moon.

The place seemed to be a small writing room. There was a bureau at the end near the window, closed, a square, Cubist-looking chair before it. The black and gold walls were bare. There was a closed bookcase, a low stool of Arab workmanship, and the narrow settee upon which I had been placed.

I contrived to get to the window.

It overlooked a neglected garden . . . and at the end of the garden I saw the Canal!

Dropping into the chair, I began to taste that most bitter of all draughts which poor humanity knows—despair. I remembered Nayland Smith's story of the house at el-Khârga: . . . "A Buddhist-like resignation was threatening me more and more. . . ."

Nayland Smith!

Whilst I sat here, a fiery furnace raging within, but nevertheless useless as any snared rabbit, he was walking into a death trap!

She would have no mercy. I had seen how she dealt with those who crossed her: I had read his sentence in her glittering eyes. This time, there would be no "sporting gesture." And I . . . I should awake somewhere in China, as a male concubine of this Eastern Circe!

I bent down, resting my throbbing head on the bureau. . . .

Then came sounds.

Somewhere a bell rang. There were voices. I heard movements—I divined that the house door had been opened and that some heavy burden had been carried in.

The sounds died away. Silence fell again.

How long I sat there, in a dreadful apathy, I had no means of judging. But suddenly the door was unlocked, and I started up.

Fah Lo Suee came in, carrying a long-bladed knife.

§6

SHE stood watching me.

"Well?" I said. "What are you waiting for?"

She smiled, that one-sided voluptuous smile which was never reflected in her eyes; then:

"I am waiting," she replied—her bell-like voice very soft —"to try to guess what you will do when I release you."

She came forward, bent so that her small, shapely head almost rested on my shoulder, and cut the lashings which confined my wrists. Her left hand grasped my arm as she stooped. Dropping to her knees, with two strokes of the keen blade she cut away the ropes binding my ankles.

Then she stood upright, very near to me, and met my stare challengingly.

"Well?" she said in mockery.

My first impulse—for I had been thinking about Nayland Smith almost continuously—was to be read in my glance.

"It can never happen twice to me, Shan," said Fah Lo Suee.

She called a name.

The door opened—and I saw the giant Nubian looking in.

Fah Lo Suee gave a brief order. The Negro retired, closing the door.

"Does no more *subtle* method occur to you?" she asked, her voice softer than ever. "I am as ready to be lied to as any other woman, Shan—by the right man—if he only tells his lies sweetly."

And, face to face with this evilly beautiful woman, knowing, as I knew too well, that my own life was at

Dr. Amber | 175

stake, that possibly I could even bargain for that of Nayland Smith, I asked myself—why not? With her own lips she had reminded me of that old adage, "all's fair in love and war." With her it was love—or the only sort of love she knew; with me it was war. Perhaps, on a scruple, hung the fate of nations!

She drew a step nearer. The perfumed aura of her personality began to envelop me. Choice was being filched from the bargain. Those mad urgings which I had known in the green-gold room in Limehouse began to beat upon my brain.

I clenched my fists. I could possibly buy the safety of the Western world with a kiss! Tensed fingers relaxed. In another instant my arms would have been around that slender, yielding body; when:

"Greville!" came a distant cry. "*Greville!*"

And I knew the voice!

I sprang back from Fah Lo Suee as from a poised cobra. Her face changed. It was as though a mask had been dropped. I saw Kâli—the patronne of assassins. . . .

She snapped her fingers.

Before I could move further, collect my scattered thoughts, the Nubian was on me!

I got in one straight right, perfectly timed. It didn't even check him. . . .

As his Herculean grip deprived me of all power of movement, Fah Lo Suee turned and went out. She hissed an order.

The Nubian threw me face downward on the settee. Never, in the whole of my experience of rough-houses, had I been so handled. I was helpless as a rat in the grip of a bull terrier. My knowledge of boxing as well as a smattering of jiu-jitsu were about as useful as botany!

I honestly believe he could have broken any normally strong man across his knee.

One of the ghastly Burmans, with the mark of Kâli on his forehead, came to assist. I was trussed up like a chicken, tossed onto the Negro's mighty shoulder, and carried from the room.

This was the end.

I had played my hand badly. On me the ultimate issue

had rested . . . and I had failed. That swift revulsion, at sound of my name—that sudden, irrational reversion to type—had sealed the doom of . . . how many?

Helpless, a mere inanimate bundle, I was carried down to the room where the image of Kâli sat on a lacquer cabinet.

The Nubian threw me roughly on the divan, so that I had no view beyond that of the lacquer cabinet and the wall against which it stood. He withdrew. I heard the closing of a door.

I turned. . . .

In the big, carved chair which formerly I had occupied, Nayland Smith was firmly lashed! There were bloodstains on his collar.

"Sir Denis! How did you know *I* was here?"

He glanced down at the coffee table.

"You left your cigarette case!" he replied. "I shouted for you—but, a Dacoit"—he indicated the bloodstains—"silenced me."

I stared at him. No words came.

"Weymouth and Yale," he went on, and the tone of his voice struck the death-knell of lingering hope, "are watching the *wrong house*. I have made my last mistake, Greville."

12 LORD OF THE SI FAN

"I THOUGHT I had found a secret base of operations," said Nayland Smith. "It's one I have used before—the house of Dr. Murray who bought Petrie's practice years ago. Evidently it's been known for some time past that I employed it in this way. I discovered—too late—that a parlourmaid in Murray's service is a spy. She doesn't know the real identity of her employers, but she has been none the less useful to them . . ."

As he spoke, he was studying every detail of the room

in which we lay trapped. Apparently he had accepted his fastenings as immovable; and evidently divining my thoughts:

"These lashings are the work of a Sea-Dyak," he explained—"palpably a specialist. Though seemingly simple, no one except the late Houdini could hope to escape from them."

"A fellow with the *mark* on his forehead? He tied *me* up! I mistook him for Burmese!"

Nayland Smith shook his head irritably.

"A member of the murder group—yes. But no Burman. He belongs to Borneo. . . . The story of my stupidity, Greville, for which so many may be called upon to pay a ghastly price, is a short one. Yale brought me a clue to-day. Its history doesn't matter—now. It was a fake. But it consisted of fragments of torn-up correspondence written in Chinese and a few cipher notes in another hand. I grappled with it: no easy task. But by about four o'clock I saw daylight. I phoned Weymouth to stand by between six and seven."

"He told me so."

"Yale also was in touch. At six o'clock I had got all the facts—including an address in Finchley Road; and at six-thirty I called Weymouth at the Park Avenue giving him full instructions. I arranged to meet him outside Lord's at half-past nine to-night.

"By a sheer accident, ten minutes later, I caught Palmer, the parlourmaid, at the telephone. Murray was in his consulting room, and there was nothing in itself remarkable about the girl's presence at the phone. She makes appointments and receives patients.

"But I heard *my own name* mentioned!

"I taxed her—and she got muddled. She was clever enough to wriggle out of the difficulty, verbally; but I had become gravely suspicious. Bearing this in mind, Greville, it's all the less excusable that I should have fallen into the trap planted for me.

"Murray's house overlooks a common, and it's usually safe to trust to picking up a taxi on the main road, although sometimes one has to wait. During dinner I said nothing about Palmer, being still in two minds as to her complicity. But when I left, I made a blunder for which I should certainly condemn the rawest recruit.

"The door of Murray's house opens on a side turning—and as I came out a taxi, proceeding slowly in the direction of the common, passed me. The man looked out as I came down the steps, and slowed up. I counted it a stroke of luck, said 'Lord's cricket ground—main entrance' —and jumped in."

Nayland Smith smiled. It was not the genial, revealing smile that I knew.

"End of story!" he added. "The windows were unopenable. As I closed the door, which locked automatically, a charge of gas was puffed into the interior. That taxi, Greville, had been waiting for me!"

"Then Weymouth and Yale—"

"Weymouth and Yale, with a Flying Squad party, are covering the house of some perfectly harmless citizen in Finchley Road! What they'll do when I fail to turn up, I can't say. But they haven't a ghost of a clue to this place —wherever it is!"

"It's beside the Regent Canal," I replied slowly. "That's all I know about it."

"Quite sufficient," he rapped. "In your amazing interview with Li King Su I detect our only ray of hope. . . ."

§2

AN INTERRUPTION came. Dimly, for sounds were muffled in this room, I heard the ringing of a bell. I saw Nayland Smith start. We both listened. We had not long to wait for the next development.

Into the room the huge Nubian came running—followed by the man whom I knew now to be a Dyak. They swept down upon Nayland Smith!

I became tongue-tied. Horror had robbed me of speech.

The man with the mark of Kâli on his brow bent swiftly. I tugged at my bonds. Nayland Smith caught my glance.

"Don't worry, Greville," he said. "A hasty removal of prisoners is evidently—"

The Nubian clapped a huge black hand over the speaker's mouth!

I saw Nayland Smith, released from the chair, but re-bound by the Dyak expert, lifted in the grasp of the giant Negro. He carried Sir Denis as he might have carried a toy dog under one arm—but he kept his free hand pressed to the captive's mouth.

There came a breathless interval. That dim ringing was renewed. The devotee of Kâli considered me, his eyes lascivious with murder. Then, as the ringing persisted, he grasped my bound ankles, jerked me to the carpet, and dragged me out of the room!

Where, formerly, I had been carried up, now I was hauled down and down, until I knew I was in the cellars of the house.

That I arrived there without sprained wrists or a cracked skull was something of a miracle. Arms fastened behind me, I had nevertheless done all I could to protect my head as I was dragged down many steps to the base-ment.

Into some dark, paved place, I was finally bundled. I divined, rather than knew, that Nayland Smith lay be-side me.

"Sir Denis," I gasped.

Wiry fingers gripped my throat, squeezing me to silence; but:

"Here!" Smith replied.

The word was cut off shortly—significantly.

There came a stirring up above—a sound of voices—of movement . . . shuffling.

My brain began to work rapidly, despite all the mal-treatment my skull had received. This was an unexpected visit of some kind! The house was being cleared of its noxious elements, of its prisoners; made presentable for inspection!

Possibly—the thought set my heart hammering—Wey-mouth, after all, had secured some clue which had led him here.

I listened intently.

Short, regular breathing almost in my ear warned me that the slightest sound on my part would result in that strangle grip being renewed.

Yes! It was the police!

There were heavy footsteps in the lobby above—deep voices.

Those sounds died away.

I told myself that the search party had gone up to explore the higher floors—and I wondered who was posing as owner of the house—and what had been done with the body of Li King Su.

The cellar in which I lay possessed drum-like properties. I distinctly heard heavy footsteps on the stairs—descending.

Perhaps the searchers had been satisfied! Perhaps they were about to go!

Louder grew the footsteps . . . louder . . .

Then, I heard, and recognized, a deep voice—

Weymouth!

At that, I determined to risk all.

A significant choking sound which came from the darkness behind might have warned me—for, even as I opened my mouth, a lean, oily smelling hand covered it—a steely grip was on my throat! . . .

"I trust you are satisfied, Inspector?" I heard, in a quavering female voice. "If there is anything else—"

"Nothing further, madam, thank you!" . . . *Weymouth!* . . . "Evidently she didn't come here. I can only apologize for troubling you."

Receding footsteps . . . murmurs of conversation.

The bang of a street door!

My head dropped back limply as the deathly grip was removed; a whisper came out of the darkness:

"A divine accident—*wasted!*"

Nayland Smith was the speaker . . . and I knew that that indomitable spirit was very near to despair.

What possibly could have led Weymouth here? Clearly, he had no information to justify a detailed search; no warrant. "Evidently *she* didn't come here. . . ." In those words the clue lay. And who was the old woman of the quavering voice?

Rapidly, these reflections flashed through my mind —but uppermost was a sense of such bitter, hopeless disappointment as I had never known before.

Truly, it was Fate.

Perhaps, as Fah Lo Suee believed, as Li King Su had believed, the day of the West was ended; perhaps we were obstacles in the way of some cataclysmic change, ordained, inevitable—and so must be brushed aside.

When presently we found ourselves back in that room where the figure of Kâli sat, immutable, on a lacquer dais, I told myself that nothing which could happen now could stir me from this dreadful apathy into which I was fallen. And, as had been the case so often in my dealings with this fiendish group, I was wrong.

From my place on the divan I stared across at Nayland Smith where he sat limply in the armchair. Then I looked quickly around.

Some time before I had suspected the tall lacquer cabinet—because of its resemblance to one I remembered at Abbots Hold—of being a concealed door. I had imagined that the figure of Kâli which surmounted it was moving. I had been right.

The masked door opened and Fah Lo Suee came in.

She wore black gloves, carried a white silk shawl, a lace cap, and a pair of spectacles! . . . Her smile was mocking.

I might have known—from her uncanny power of mastering languages and dialects—who the "old woman" had been!

"A difficult moment, Shan," she said composedly. "Something I had not foreseen or provided for. A keener brain—such as yours, Sir Denis—might have challenged the gloves, even in the case of a very eccentric old lady!"

She began to pull them off, revealing those beautiful, long, feline hands.

"But my hands are rather memorable," she added, without hint of vanity and simply as a statement of fact. "A late but expected guest was traced here. Fortunately, the taxi driver upon whose evidence the visit was made was uncertain of the number. But it was very clever of the superintendent—following a telephone call from the lady's last address—to find the man who had driven her from the station."

She turned her long, narrow eyes in Nayland Smith's

direction . . . and I saw his jaw harden as he clenched his teeth. I know, now, that already he *understood*.

"I respect you so much, Sir Denis," she went on, "that I know your removal is vital to my council. But I promise you it shall be swift."

Nayland Smith remained silent.

"A traitor has already paid the price which we demand. When Li King Su and yourself are found together—the inference will be obvious. And I have arranged for you to be found at the Limehouse end of the Canal."

Then Sir Denis spoke.

"Congratulations," he said. "You wear the cloak of your lamented father gracefully."

Perhaps some shade of emotion passed swiftly across the impassive face of Fah Lo Suee; perhaps I only imagined it. But she continued without pause:

"For you, Shan, I have pleasant duties in China—where I must return immediately, my work here undone." Again she stared at Nayland Smith. "But I am not greedy, Shan, and you shall not be lonely."

She clapped her hands.

The door from the lobby opened. . . .

And Rima was pushed into the room by the Nubian!

§ 3

OVER those first few moments that followed, I must leave a veil. Exactly what took place I shall never know. The shock of it stupefied me.

". . . They said you were ill, Shan. . . . I came right away without waiting to speak to a soul. . . ."

Those words reached me through a sort of drumming in my head. Now I saw Rima's grave eyes turn to Fah Lo Suee in such a look of loathing horror as I had never seen in them before.

But Fah Lo Suee met that glance without animosity. In her own strange eyes of jade green there was no glint of feminine triumph, no mockery. Only a calm consideration. She had mocked Nayland Smith, she had mocked me: we were her active potent enemies, and she had outwitted us. Rima she regarded with something strangely like a cold compassion.

That God had ever given life to a woman so far above the weaknesses of her sex as Fah Lo Suee was something I could never have believed without convincing evidence. Even her curious infatuation for myself was a mere feline fancy, ordered and contained. She would have sacrificed nothing to it; nor would it long outlast its realization.

"Shan!" Rima's voice suddenly rose to a high emotional note; she moved forward. "Tell me—"

"Be silent, child," said Fah Lo Suee. "Sit there."

She indicated an armchair. Rima's despairing glance met mine; then she obeyed that quiet, imperious command. Fah Lo Suee signalled to the Nubian to go. He withdrew, not wholly closing the door.

"Shan attracts me," Fah Lo Suee went on. "Apart from which he has qualities which will prove useful when we move in Egypt. But I don't want to steal him from you" —she glanced at Rima—"and he would be unhappy without you."

We were all watching her. There was absolute silence in the room when she ceased speaking. Of the many violent scenes I had known from that dark hour when Sir Lionel's voice—or so I had supposed at the time— called out to me in the wâdi where we were camped, this quiet, deadly interlude before the amazement to come recurs most frequently in my memory.

"It is very simple, Shan"—she turned to me. "Sir Denis has checked me—would always check me. He knows too much of our plans. So do you. The others can wait. If Superintendent Weymouth had come here *alone*—he would have remained. . . . After you have gone . . . he will become dangerous. But he must wait.

"His arrival here to-night was an unfortunate accident —due to my consideration of your happiness."

I met the steady gaze of those enthralling eyes. . . . "Your happiness . . ." As though, unwittingly, she had communicated her secret thoughts to me, I grasped the truth; I saw the part that Rima was to play. *I*, alone, might prove difficult. Rima, helpless in the power of Fah Lo Suee, would make me a pliant slave! Suddenly:

"More and more," said Nayland Smith, "I regret the

absence of Dr. Fu Manchu. I would rather deal with *him* than with his daughter!"

Fah Lo Suee turned, suddenly.

"Why do you assume my father to be dead?" she asked.

Nayland Smith exchanged a rapid glance with me; then:

"I don't assume anything of the kind," he rapped, with all his old vigour. "I know he's alive!"

"How do you know?"

"That is *my* business. Kindly confine yourself to a statement of your own."

There were some moments of silence; then:

"Dr. Fu Manchu," said Fah Lo Suee, "is alive—yes. You were always a clever man, Sir Denis. But his age prohibits travel."

I dared not trust myself to look at Nayland Smith. It was incredible.

She didn't know that Fu Manchu was in England!

Smith made no reply.

"The work that he laid down," Fah Lo Suee went on, "I have taken up. The *Si Fan*, Sir Denis, is a power again. But time is precious. The unforeseen visit of Superintendent Weymouth delayed me. There are only two members in England now. They are in this house. They will leave with me. . . . Shan, do you choose that yourself and Rima shall travel as baggage, or will you bow to—the inevitable?"

"Agree!" rapped Nayland Smith. "A hundred chances of helping the world present themselves to a live man—but not to a synthetic corpse."

"Shan!"

Rima, wild-eyed, was staring at me. She had sprung up from her chair.

"What?" I asked dully.

"I don't know the meaning of it all—I can only guess; but you wouldn't *bargain*, Shan?"

Nayland Smith caught my wandering glance, and:

"He would, Rima," he answered. "So would I—if I had the chance! Don't be foolish, little lady. This isn't a game of tennis. It's a game of which you don't know the rules. There's only one thing to play for . . . life. Because, while one of us lives, there's always a chance that one may win!—Agree, Greville! It's nine thousand miles to China—and with two active brains alert, anything may happen."

I closed my eyes. This was agony. An age seemed to pass. Had Nayland Smith some scheme behind his words? And where did my duty lie? . . . My duty to Rima; my duty to the world. . . .

"I will agree," I said at last—and my voice was one I could never have recognized, "on the distinct understanding that Rima is not to be harmed or molested in any way—and that Sir Denis is released to-night."

Opening my eyes, I glanced quickly at Fah Lo Suee. Her expression was inscrutable. I looked at Rima. She was staring at me—an uncomprehending stare. . . . Lastly, I looked at Nayland Smith.

His steely eyes regarded me wistfully. He twisted his lips in a wry grimace and shook his head, as:

"Your second condition is impossible," Fah Lo Suee replied.

And as she spoke the miracle happened; the thing of which to this very hour I sometimes doubt the reality, seeming, as it does now, rather part of a fevered dream than an actual occurrence.

I don't know what prompted me, as that bell-like voice ceased, to look again at Rima. But I did so.

She was staring past me—at the lacquer cabinet where Kâli sat—the hidden doorway Fah Lo Suee had closed again.

I twisted around.

Very slowly—inch by inch—inch by inch—the door was opening! Then, suddenly, it was opened wide. Out of the darkness beyond two figures came; first, the Dyak, who, instant on entering the room, turned again to the lacquered door and dropped on his knees; second, the Nubian—who also prostrated himself!

Thirdly, and last, came a figure whose image must remain imprinted on my mind for ever. . . .

It was that of a very tall old man; emaciated to a degree which I had hitherto associated only with mummies. His great height was not appreciable at first glance, by reason of the fact that he stooped very much, resting his weight on a stout stick. He wore a plain black garment, resembling a cassock, and a little black cap was set on his head. . . .

His skull—his fleshless yellow skull—was enormous. I thought that such a brain must be that either of a madman or of a genius. And his face, a map of wrinkles, resembled nothing so much as the shrivelled majesty of the Pharaoh Seti I who lives in the Cairo Museum!

Deeply sunken eyes emitted a dull green spark.

But this frail old man radiated such *power* that I was chilled—it seemed to be physical; I could not have experienced a more dreadful sense of impotent horror if the long-dead Pharaoh himself had appeared before me. . . .

Those sunken, commanding eyes ignored my existence. Their filmy but potent regard passed the grovelling men, passed me, and was set upon Fah Lo Suee. Then came a sibilant command, utterly beyond my powers to describe:

"*Kneel*, little thief! *I* am standing . . ."

I twisted around.

Fah Lo Suee, a chalky quality tingeing the peach bloom of her skin, had lowered that insolent head! As I turned, staring, *she dropped to her knees!*

And now I saw that Nayland Smith, bound as he was, arms and ankles, had got to his feet. Through the tropical yellow of his complexion, through the artificial stain which still lingered, he had paled.

The hissing voice spoke again.

"Greeting, Sir Denis. Be seated."

Smith's teeth were clenched so hard that his jaw muscles stood out lumpishly. But, relaxing and speaking in a low, even tone:

"Greeting," he replied, "Dr. Fu Manchu."

§ 4

THREE times, heavily, Dr. Fu Manchu beat his stick upon the floor.

Two Burmans came in and saluted him.

I knew them. They were the Dacoits who had been present at the Council of Seven in el-Khârga.

Dr. Fu Manchu advanced into the room. Extending a

bony, clawlike hand, he indicated the kneeling Fah Lo Suee.

And, without word or glance, eyes lowered, Fah Lo Suee went out with her dreadful escort! It was in my heart to pity her, so utterly was she fallen, so slavishly did that proud woman bow her head to this terrible, imperious old man.

As he passed the prostrate figures of the Nubian and the Dyak, walking heavily and slowly, he touched them each with his stick. He spoke in a low voice, gutturally.

They sprang up and approached Rima!

Throughout this extraordinary scene, which had passed much more quickly than its telling conveys, Rima had remained seated—stupefied. Now, realizing the meaning of Fu Manchu's last order, she stood up—horror in her eyes.

"Shan! Shan!" she cried. "What is he going to do to me?"

Dr. Fu Manchu beat upon the floor again and spoke one harsh word. The Nubian and the Dyak stood still. No sergeant of the Guards ever had more complete control of men.

"Miss Barton," he said, his voice alternating uncannily between the sibilant and the guttural and seeming to be produced with difficulty, "your safety is assured. I wish to be alone with Sir Denis and Mr. Greville. For your greater ease, Sir Denis will tell you that my word is my bond."

He turned those sunken, filmed eyes in the direction of the big armchair and:

"You needn't worry, Rima," said Nayland Smith. "Dr. Fu Manchu guarantees your safety."

I was amazed beyond reason. Even so fortified, Rima's eyes were dark with terror. A swift flow of words brought the Dyak sharply about to take his instructions. Then he and the Nubian escorted Rima from the room.

I tugged, groaning, at the cords which held me. I stared at Nayland Smith. Was he holding a candle to the devil? How could a sane man accept the assurances of such a proven criminal?

But, as though my ideas had been spoken aloud:

"Do not misjudge Sir Denis," came the harsh voice. "He knows that in warfare I am remorseless. But he knows also that no mandarin of my order has ever willingly broken his promise."

The Nubian had closed the door leading to the lobby. Dr. Fu Manchu had closed that of the false cabinet as he came into the room. No sound entered the arena where this menace to white supremacy and the man whose defenses had defied him confronted one another.

§5

"It is a strange fact," said Dr. Fu Manchu, "that only the circumstance of your being a prisoner allows of our present conversation."

He paused, watching, watching Nayland Smith with those physically weak but spiritually powerful eyes. The Chinaman's *force* was incredible. It was as though a great lamp burned in that frail, angular body.

"Yet, now, by a paradox, we stand together."

Resting on his ebony stick, he drew himself up so that his thin frame assumed something of its former height.

"My methods are not your methods. Perhaps I have laughed at your British scruples. Perhaps a day may come, Sir Denis, when you will join in my laughter. But, as much as I have hated you, I have always admired your clarity of mind and your tenacity. You were instrumental in defeating me, when I had planned to readjust the centre of world power. No doubt you thought me mad—a megalomaniac. You were wrong."

He spoke the last three words in a low voice—almost a whisper.

"I worked for my country. I saw China misruled, falling into decay; with all her vast resources, becoming prey for carrion. I hoped to give China that place in the world to which her intellect, her industry, and her ideals entitle her. I hoped to *awaken* China. My methods, Sir Denis, were bad. My motive was good."

His voice rose. He raised one gaunt hand in a gesture of defiance. Nayland Smith spoke no word. And I watched this wraith of terror as one watches a creature uncreated, who figures hideously in some disordered dream. His sincerity was unmistakable; his power of intellect enormous. But when I realized *what* he defended, what he stood for—and that I, Shan Greville, was listening to him in a house somewhere in Regent's Park, I felt like laughing hysterically. . . .

"Your long reign, Sir Denis, is ending. A blacker tragedy than any I had dreamt of will end your Empire. It is Fate that both of us must now look on. I thank my gods that the consummation will not be seen by me.

"The woman you know as Fah Lo Suee—it was her pet name in nursery days—is my child by a Russian mother. In her, Sir Denis, I share the sorrow of Shakespeare's King Lear. . . . She has reawakened a power which I had buried. I cannot condemn her. She is my flesh. But in China we expect, and *exact*, obedience. The *Si Fan* is a society older than Buddhism and more flexible. Its ruler wields a sword none can withstand. For many years *Si Fan* has slumbered. Fah Lo Suee has dared to awaken it!"

He turned his dreadful eyes on me for the first time since he had begun to speak.

"Mr. Greville, you cannot know what control of that organization means! *Misdirected*, at such a crisis of history as this, it could only mean another world war! I dragged myself from retirement"—he looked again at Nayland Smith—"to check the madness of Fah Lo Suee. Some harm she has done. But I have succeeded. To-night, again, I am lord of the *Si Fan!*"

Quivering, he rested on his stick.

"I had never dreamt," said Nayland Smith, "that I should live to applaud your success."

Dr. Fu Manchu turned and walked to the lacquer door. Reaching it:

"If you were free," he replied, "it would be your duty to detain me. My plans are made. Fah Lo Suee will trouble you no more. Overtake me if you wish—and if you can. I am indifferent to the issue, Sir Denis, but I leave England to-night. *Si Fan* will sleep again. The balance of world power *will* be readjusted—but not as she had planned.

"In half an hour I will cause Superintendent Weymouth—whom I esteem—to be informed that you are here. Miss Barton, during that period, must remain locked in a room above. Greeting and good-bye, Sir Denis. Greeting and good-bye, Mr. Greville."

He went out and closed the door. . . .

§6

NEARLY a year has passed since that night when for the first, and I pray for the last, time I found myself face to face with Dr. Fu Manchu—the world's greatest criminal, perhaps the world's supreme genius—and a man of his word.

Unable to credit the facts, a few minutes after his disappearance, I shouted Rima's name.

She replied—her voice reaching me dimly from some higher room. She was safe, but locked in. . . .

And an hour later, Weymouth arrived—to find Nayland Smith at last disentangled from the cunning knots of the Sea-Dyak!

"It was possible, after all, Greville! But a damned long business!"

I write these concluding notes before my tent in Sir Lionel Barton's camp on the site of ancient Nineveh. Sunset draws near, and I can see Rima, a camera slung over her shoulder, coming down the slope.

We are to be married on our return to London.

Of Dr. Fu Manchu, Fah Lo Suee, and their terrible escort, no trace was ever discovered!

Even the body of Li King Su was spirited away. Six months of intense and world-wide activity, directed by Nayland Smith, resulted in . . . nothing! "My plans are made," that great and evil man had said.

Sometimes I doubt if it ever happened. Sometimes I wonder if it is really finished. Before me, on the box which is my extemporized writing desk, lies a big emerald set in an antique silver ring. It reached me only a month ago in a package posted from Hong Kong. There was no note inside. . . .